MONTANA MINE

A SMALL TOWN ROMANCE - BOOK 5

VANESSA VALE

D1496348

Montana Mine

ISBN: 978-1-7959-0013-3

Copyright © 2018 by Vanessa Vale

Cover design: Bridger Media

Cover graphic: Deposit Photos: Sofia_Zhuvarets, photocreo

GET A FREE BOOK!

JOIN MY MAILING LIST TO BE THE
FIRST TO KNOW OF NEW RELEASES,
FREE BOOKS, SPECIAL PRICES AND
OTHER AUTHOR GIVEAWAYS.

http://freeromanceread.com

PROLOGUE

I was usually very rational, very sane. Growing up with a crazy aunt, I hadn't had much choice. When my Halloween costume in Kindergarten was a perfect replica of a stapler and not a fairy princess, my five-year-old brain had known something was fishy. When I found two hard boiled eggs floating in water dyed yellow in a second-hand pickle jar for lunch in fourth grade, it had been time to make my own lunch. Then there was the middle school dance, when she'd gone not just as chaperone but as the principal's date, and they were caught together in a very compromising position in the janitor's closet. Needless to say, the man had relocated to Florida, and I knew I needed to get out of town. I couldn't compete with Aunt Velma.

To say that my aunt was famous in town—perhaps infamous was a better word—was an understatement. Being known as 'Velma Dinkweiler's niece', not Daphne Lane, spoke volumes about our two personalities. That was why one day in July, I lost it. Completely and totally lost it. Maybe the fruit didn't fall as far from the tree as people had thought.

1

Maybe my parents left me on Aunt Velma's doorstep because they knew I would turn out as crazy as she was. Maybe I was just a late bloomer and had to grow into my craziness. Whatever the reason, looking back, crazy might not be so bad after all.

CHAPTER 1

"*M*a'am, I'm Detective McCade. I need to see your license and registration."

Detective McCade? Make that Detective McHottie. Yeah, it wasn't his name, but it fit and so did his jeans and black t-shirt. He was tall, tall enough where I could only see a very specific portion of his body from my vantage point—a very nice portion of a pair of well-worn jeans molded in *all* the right places. I shouldn't get a hot flash at this point in my life, but yup, this guy was working for me. I licked my lips.

He had to bend at the waist, a forearm resting on the roof of my car, to look at me through the open window. His hair was cut short, but I could see how it would curl if it grew out a bit. His jaw was square and clean shaven, his nose had a slight crook in it, which could mean he had a little bit of fight beneath the law enforcement. His eyes were shielded by mirrored sunglasses, so I dreamed that he had blue eyes. A little Black Irish to go with his Scot name. A service pistol was clipped to his belt along with a badge which made the whole snug jeans thing even hotter. He pretty much looked like a GI Joe action figure minus the army fatigues.

"Hey, you're Silky Tangles." He grinned, and it was his turn to lick his lips.

I frowned. "Excuse me?"

"Silky Tangles, the um...film star."

I handed over my license. "Yeah, um...no. No Silky Tangles here, unless you're referring to my hair which sometimes does get tangled, the curls and all. Silky? I guess that's a compliment, right?"

He looked at my ID. "Daphne Lane," he read. "Not very catchy. I guess you do need a better name than that for your line of work."

"Hey!" I felt slightly insulted, but I was too confused to know how to retort. Who the heck was Silky Tangles? "Look, how do I know you're a real police officer? You don't really act like one with the tangled hair comment and all."

He had a Kojak light on the dash of his SUV, not a police cruiser, but I was law-abiding enough to know when to pull over. Perhaps not law-abiding enough to keep to the speed limit. Sometimes a girl's got to do what a girl's got to do. And I had to catch my flight.

"Ma'am?" he asked, his eyebrows going up above his sunglasses.

"I've seen on *Dateline* where women are taken and cut up into little pieces by a man who pretends to be a police officer." I wouldn't mind being taken by McHottie, skipping the cutting up part.

"Ma'am, it's ten o'clock on a Tuesday in Montana. Not four in the morning in downtown Detroit. I pulled you over because you were going ninety in a forty-five."

He did have a point. I had been going fast. I leaned across the center console to reach the glove box for the registration. "Look, Officer—"

"Detective," he countered.

"Detective," I repeated, blowing hair out of my eyes. "I'm

4

trying to make a flight. I've got an hour until it takes off." I turned back to face him, held out the paper for him to take. He lifted his chin a few inches. Had he been checking out my ass?

"Where are you headed?" His t-shirt afforded me a very nice view of tanned forearms with corded muscles sprinkled with dark hair. No wedding ring. A thirty-year-old woman noticed these types of things even when the man was keeping her from her next assignment. It wasn't like I planned to linger and have his babies. Men were the antichrist at the moment, even hot ones, but that didn't mean I didn't take a moment to ogle.

"Thailand."

He shook his head as he looked at my license photo, then at me. It was not the best picture—whose was? I'd had a moment of inspiration and cut my bangs, but seeing the photo at the DMV only confirmed I'd made a serious error in judgment. My brown hair was too curly for bangs and I could only imagine what McHottie thought.

"Look, Miss Lane, I've heard a lot of excuses for speeding, but Thailand? You couldn't come up with something better than that? Besides, I thought films like yours were now done in the valley."

"The valley? Gallatin Valley?" Bozeman was situated in a flat, open plain between three sets of mountain ranges, also known as the Gallatin Valley. What was he talking about? I narrowed my eyes. He doubted me? "Oh. You don't think I'm going to Thailand? What should I have said instead?"

"Going into labor is used frequently." His gaze raked over my body with that revelation. "Yeah, that one won't work for you. You need to keep your body in tip-top shape." He waggled his eyebrows and actually grinned. Of course, he had a dimple.

I didn't know if I should be flattered, annoyed or grossed

out. "I don't have time for this," I snapped. I could feel my anger building. Patience had never been one of my strong suits, perhaps stifled from dealing with Aunt Velma all my life. One would think I'd become *more* patient because of her antics, but no. Definitely not. I didn't have a patient bone in my body. That's why I was a travel journalist and didn't have to wait for anyone. Except for Officer, no, Detective McHottie, to hand me my ticket so I could speed even more to get to the airport in time. "I really am going to Thailand, although if I miss my flight, I won't even make it as far as Salt Lake and will miss the Ubon Ratchathani Candle Festival. Can you *please* give me my ticket so I can be on my way?"

"Wait here." He stood up and looking at my side mirror I watched him head back to his car. Yeah, the pants fit him just fine. I drummed my fingers on the steering wheel, the impatience building with every second. I'd only returned to Bozeman for Aunt Velma's birthday as I'd had a week off between assignments. Montana wasn't on the way to anything, so the flight choices to Thailand were limited. As it was, I had to go to Salt Lake City, then Chicago, then Narita, Japan, to connect to Bangkok. It would take over twenty-four hours to get there and missing one flight would mean I missed them all. And I'd lose my assignment. If I lost the story, I didn't get paid. I was freelance, which meant the next job wasn't guaranteed. Since Roger turned out to be a little shit and decided to shack up with someone else, someone who liked Shalimar perfume and red patent fuck-me heels, I needed the cash to find a new place to live. At least, a new place to crash. Travel journalism didn't allow for Home Sweet Home.

I watched the clock on my dash. Fiddled with the radio. Dug out twelve cents between the seat and the center console. Five, ten minutes and the man just sat in his car. He was looking down, but he could have been doing anything from writing up my ticket to playing a game of Solitaire on his cell phone. *Come on!*

When I had twenty minutes left to get on the flight before they gave my seat away, I'd had enough. I climbed from my old VW Rabbit to tell the man to get a move on. As I approached, he glanced up from his seat, opened his car door and stepped out. He was a few inches over six feet and must have eaten his Wheaties for breakfast to turn out like he did.

"I'm not exactly sure what you're doing in there, but it can't take that long to write a ticket." I just shook my head in disappointment. My friend Violet was a first-grade teacher and I'd seen her use the look before. It worked on six-year olds and adults alike.

Not this guy. I could tell from his stance and how he had one hand on top of the gun at his hip while holding some weird black thing in his other that I may have done the wrong thing. "Ma'am, you need to get back in your car."

I held up my hands in the 'don't shoot' position. "Just give me my ticket and I'll go."

"Ma'am, you need to get back in your car now or I'm going to have to cuff you. You know what it's like, from your third film, *Cuffed and Stuffed.*"

My hands dropped, so did my mouth. "Are you kidding me?" *Cuffed and Stuffed?* It sounded like a porno. What was wrong with this guy? "You're going to cuff me? If you hadn't taken so long, I wouldn't be standing here right now. I *need* to get on that plane. It's not like I tried to talk my way out of the ticket. I've even asked for it."

I could see one eyebrow raise. "Thailand? Seriously? You're dressed for yoga class and let me tell you, all that stretching pays off on screen." He may have winked, but the glasses hid it well.

I think my head exploded then because his eyes widened —I could tell even through the mirrored glasses—and he took a half step back. His hand clenched around the butt of the gun.

"Do you know what it's like to come back here? Do you have *any* idea what I've been through this week? What will happen if I miss that flight? And you're standing here discussing my flexibility?"

"Ma'am, I need you to turn around and place your hands on the roof of your car." He stepped closer. I stepped back. "A police cruiser will be here in a few minutes to give you your ticket."

"A few minutes?" I started waving my arms around as I spoke. "No. I'm going to Thailand. I *need* to go to Thailand. I can't spend another night as a designated driver for a bunch of senior citizens. I can't fill in again for league bowling just to get my ass pinched by Frank Zajik. And if I have to spend another night listening to a borderline geriatric couple getting it on when I'm in the Sahara Desert of a sex life, I might do something crazy. Give me my stupid ticket."

I might have seen his lip twitch in amusement, or it could have been a nervous tick.

"Sahara Desert? Yeah, right. I thought you said Thailand. Ma'am, have you been drinking?"

I screeched so loudly birds flew off out of the field beside the road. The last thing I remember about Detective McHottie before the world went black was that he had a little scar in his left eyebrow.

CHAPTER 2

"*D*aphne." I heard my name through a fog, my brain not able to make any of my body parts work. Including my eyes. "Really, Carl, a stun gun?" It sounded like Aunt Velma, but everything was confusing. Why couldn't I wiggle my toes?

"McCade says she went crazy and punched him."

Ah, I could feel my fingertips.

"That doesn't sound like Daphne," Aunt Velma replied.

My whole body jerked all at once, as if my brain and my muscles finally decided to become friends again.

"There, she's coming to now. We can get her side of the story," the man offered.

I was able to control my eyes, which might not have been a good thing, because the first thing I saw was Aunt Velma's generous cleavage. She knelt beside where I was lying and sighed in relief, her bosom heaving as she did so. She was sixty-five, had hair dyed fire engine red and wore makeup in a way only a Mary Kay consultant or a Texas housewife could pull off successfully. Her shirt was also fire engine red with a plunging V neckline, leaving little to the imagination.

Behind her, the walls were cinderblock and painted white. Fluorescent bulbs cast a harsh white light.

Sitting up carefully, I pushed my hair back from my face and realized where I was. Jail. The little metal toilet built into the wall was the giveaway. The concrete bed—if that was the word for it—was very hard and very cold beneath me. The smell of institutional strength cleaning products and something else I didn't even want to consider was strong in the small room. Rubbing my face, I tried to get my brain synapses working again. "What happened?" I muttered, wiping a copious amount of drool off my chin.

"Stun gun," Aunt Velma muttered. She rose from her crouch on the floor and stood tall in front of me. My aunt had been described in many ways including big-boned and an Amazon, or a big-boned Amazon. Both were valid, but to me she looked more like the retired roller derby queen that she was. She epitomized the big hair, tight spandex with no bra combination, and no holds barred behavior. She hadn't changed much from the picture of her on the fireplace mantel from her lengthy stint with the Fargo Roller Dolls from 1979, except now gravity had set in, and she'd discovered the alluring properties of a wonder bra.

No one messed with Aunt Velma. She'd been allowed to be crazy for decades and no one questioned. I go insane for five minutes and I get stun gunned and tossed in jail.

"I'm sorry about this, Daphne, but JT did say you were off your rocker."

Now that the cobwebs cleared, I knew the man standing next to Aunt Velma. Fortunately, he was wearing more clothes than just the plaid boxers I'd seen him wearing this very morning in the kitchen. Carl Dobbs was police captain and in charge of the detective squad, the one that included stun-first-ask-questions-later McCade. He was also the current man *du jour* of Aunt Velma's, and I knew more about

Carl than I ever wanted. I could personally confirm that he was not a premature ejaculator and he had the sexual endurance of a college kid in Florida on spring break. Lucky Aunt Velma. Thailand wasn't far enough to escape the horrors I'd listened to from the dynamic duo the night before.

"Off my rocker? Is that what he said?" How dare the man! No matter how hot he was. *Off my rocker.* I'd show that man off my rocker. I realized I was grumbling it aloud instead of just in my mind.

Carl looked a little apprehensive. "You...you did punch him in the face."

I punched—oh yeah, it was coming back to me now.

"Who taught you to hit like that?" Aunt Velma didn't even try to hide the pleased gleam in her eye.

"You did. Summer after tenth grade, right after Ryan Grasselmeyer got a little too frisky at the movies." She'd spent the entire Sunday morning, instead of going to church like a normal family, giving me pointers on how to make a fist and where to strike on the face.

Aunt Velma nodded, her gold hoop earrings swinging with the motion. "Right. I heard he weighs over two hundred fifty pounds now and sells used cars up in Great Falls."

"Ninety in a forty-five, Daphne, that's a little over the top, don't you think?" Carl asked, his whiskers making a rasping sound as he ran his hand over his chin.

If he'd had to listen to someone else making sounds like he and Aunt Velma had, he'd be fleeing town as quickly as possible, too.

"I overslept and was running late for my flight." I turned my gaze to Aunt Velma. "Someone kept me up half the night."

She had the gall to smile and give a furtive and flirtatious glance at Carl. "Yeah, someone kept me up half the night, too."

The man's cheeks reddened like Santa Claus'.

I groaned and stood, both Velma and Carl stepping back out of my way. "Can I get out of here now?"

Velma looked me over critically. "At least you didn't pee yourself. I've heard that's a side effect from being stunned."

I glanced down my body. Long sleeved dark blue t-shirt with Minnesota across the front, black yoga pants, old sneakers with a gray cardigan wrapped around my waist. My hair was no longer in a ponytail and was wild about my head. Other than having my brain sizzled, I didn't seem worse for wear. And I hadn't become incontinent before Aunt Velma.

"The speeding and the stun gun sort of voided each other out, so you're free to go," Carl answered. He held out his hand toward the open jail cell door and led me down the labyrinth of corridors to the lobby.

I'd missed my flight, I didn't know where my little car was, nor what I was going to do to replace the Thailand assignment. What I did know was that I was stuck in Montana with Aunt Velma until I could figure it out. I had nowhere else to go. When I'd finished my last assignment in Kiev, I'd flown back to LA for the short break until it was time to go to Thailand. On arrival, I'd found out that Roger, my boyfriend—if that was what you called a guy you hadn't seen in three months—had taken up with another woman. The term boyfriend was a very lax description of him since we barely saw each other. He was a consultant doing some kind of computer security thing and he was a road warrior, too. Our schedules never meshed. Fortunately, they hadn't meshed last week when I'd landed and found the evidence of the new cohabitation arrangement. I certainly didn't wear six-inch stilettos. So I flew to Bozeman and to Aunt Velma's, the only place I had to go. Fortunately, it coincided with her birthday, so there weren't any questions about my surprise appearance.

"Carl Dobbs, what did you do to Daphne?" The question was shouted from across the lobby of the jail. Folks who were sitting in plastic chairs bolted to the floor, most likely waiting for their turn to see an incarcerated loved one, swiveled their heads. I froze in place and took a deep breath. *Great.* The only person crazier than Aunt Velma was her best friend, Goldie West. When the two of them got together, it was like combining baking soda and vinegar in science class. A really big show with lots of fizz.

Goldie West was a force of nature. A few years older than Aunt Velma, she owned and ran the only adult store in this part of Montana. She knew everyone within a hundred-mile radius and their secrets, too. She was like a doctor, a lawyer and a priest combined. Not only did she keep people's proclivities confidential, she ensured her customers a healthy sex life, kept the city's divorce rate down and knew which folks were going to hell.

My friend Veronica, Violet's twin sister, had compared Goldie to the Tasmanian Devil. She spun in and wreaked havoc and left people stunned and confused in her wake. Her blonde hair was pulled up into a high ponytail, dangly earrings identical to Aunt Velma's hung from her ears to almost brush against her hot pink t-shirt with the word 'sassy' written in sparkly gemstones across her chest. And when she came across the lobby to join us, everything stopped. Heads turned, conversation ceased. Even the phone stopped ringing.

Veronica had worked part-time at Goldilocks ever since she became legal, so I'd been in and out of the store for years. But I'd slipped under the woman's radar for the most part because I'd spent my high school years at boarding school in Vermont, then on to Minnesota for college and then fell right into my freelance writing which kept me away from

Bozeman for long stretches of time. I loved Aunt Velma, but she was...exhausting.

"Really, Carl," Goldie tsked and shook her head. "Just look at her."

I must have looked pretty darn bad if Goldie pointed it out.

Carl looked like a little kid who'd been scolded. "I haven't done anything, Goldie, and you know it. JT McCade caught the girl going ninety and pulled her over."

"I heard he stun gunned her until she peed her pants." Goldie's eyebrow went up as she looked me over.

So did everyone else in the waiting room. Word spread in Bozeman faster than a wildfire during a drought. I rolled my eyes.

She held out a pair of pants. "Here. I brought you a pair of jeggings." She tossed them to me and I caught them without thinking. I held them up.

"They're jeans, but they're leggings. See? I'm wearing a pair, too."

Yes. Yes, she was wearing a pair of jeggings with a pair of her usual clogs. The combination prompted me to never wear the pair she'd just brought me.

"Wow, thanks, Miss Goldie, but I didn't pee my pants," I said loud enough so everyone who was listening knew that fact.

"Keep them then. It was one of those TV specials where you buy one pair and they send you the second pair for free. Good thing we wear the same size. Unlike your aunt over there who can share clothes with the MSU basketball team."

"Hey!" Aunt Velma retorted crankily. She couldn't say much more because it was true. While she was close to six feet tall, I was average. Only five and a half feet barefooted, I was so-so on the weight department. I could stand to lose a few pounds, but a donut with my name on it would not be ignored. I had average brown hair of average length, average brown eyes. I was *average*.

"Carl doesn't seem to mind that I'm big boned," Velma said.

Everyone in the room looked to Carl. He was one of a few men who made Aunt Velma look petite. He'd been a bronc busting champion four years running and had been the quarterback of MSU's football team back in the day. He'd worked first as a beat cop, but I didn't know how a police cruiser had fit him. "No, ma'am, I sure don't," he replied with a sly grin.

I wiped a hand over my eyes and looked away and directly into the face of Detective McHottie.

"Oh shit," he mumbled. Rubbing the back of his neck, he looked a little contrite. A little, which was not enough. I wanted him licking my boots, if I had them on, for making me miss my flight.

"You!" I pointed at him. "You stun gunned me!"

His dark eyebrows went up, and I could clearly see the scar that bisected the left one. "You punched me in the nose."

Yeah, his nose did look a little swollen, but it did nothing to diminish his hotness, especially now that I could see his eyes. And I'd been wrong. His eyes weren't blue, they were dark, so dark they'd be considered black. With his dark hair, holy cow. His picture was next to tall, dark and handsome in the dictionary.

Carl stepped between us, held his hands up, probably not wanting an incident in the lobby. "Everything balances out and we're going to forget this incident ever happened. Right, McCade?"

He gave a small nod, but his jaw was clenched so tight I was surprised his teeth didn't shatter.

"How can I forget?" I tossed my hands up. "I missed my flight to Thailand."

"Thailand?" McCade rolled his eyes in that way men do

when they want to piss a woman off. "You're still on that? Seriously? You're off the hook, so let it go. It's a good thing you don't talk much in those movies of yours." He cracked his knuckles.

I narrowed my eyes at him and I swear my blood pressure went to stroke point. "Off the hook? You *stun gunned* me. I woke up in a jail cell."

His gaze raked over me. My nipples tightened and the way his jaw clamped tight, he'd definitely noticed. "At least you didn't pee yourself. There's something to be said in that."

I chose to let the peeing remark go. I figured I'd covered that one by now. "What's the deal with this movie stuff? You act as if I'm some movie star or something."

He held up his hands in surrender. "If you want to keep it a secret, that's fine, but you might want to consider wearing a different shirt."

I glanced down. Yeah, my nipples were showing through the old college t-shirt. I crossed my arms over my chest with a huff. "What the hell are you talking about?" I hissed.

He leaned in and I could smell him. Soap, Montana sky and pheromones. As he got closer, I shifted back, but he was taller and I wasn't a gymnast, no matter how flexible he thought I was, so he was able to whisper in my ear. His warm breath tickled on my neck and that sent goose bumps skittering...everywhere. "Your secret's safe with me. If you don't want anyone to know where you go when you leave town, that's fine. But I know, and let me tell you, Silky Tangles is the center of my every fantasy, especially that thing she does when she's cuffed. I've got my handcuffs if you ever want to practice for the sequel."

My brain was completely repulsed by the jackass, but my body didn't care. He was hot. He made my nipples tighten by just being in the same room. I wasn't going to consider what happened to my lady parts when he'd all but licked my ear.

He pulled back a little and we just stared at each other, the corner of his mouth ticking up. His eyes were so dang dark, yet so clear. Smug.

"JT McCade, as I live and breathe. You've sure grown up. *He's* the guy you punched?" Goldie asked, which had me practically jumping back, realizing how close he'd been. Her mouth hung open in awe. Aunt Velma wasn't immune either, but Carl was right there, so she hid it pretty well. It appeared any woman in the room was affected by the man's looks. If I didn't want to taser him, I'd want to climb him like a monkey.

I whipped my head toward Goldie. "This is the guy who *stun gunned* me." I pointed my thumb over my shoulder. "How many times do I have to say it? Besides, he thinks I'm...um... well. Never mind." I didn't need to mention that he thought I was some kind of porn star who had a penchant for hand-cuffs. I just wanted to get out of here.

He raised his hand to his mouth and mimicked zipping it shut and throwing away the key.

"What are you, in first grade?" I wondered, shaking my head. He actually thought that I really hadn't been going to Thailand, but was leaving town in secret to star in porn flicks? I took a step toward him and clenched my fist, ready to slug the jerk, but, of course, Aunt Velma interceded.

"Young man, you don't want to mess with a woman who is clearly in the throes of PMS."

"Aunt Velma!" I screeched. I felt my cheeks heat from embarrassment along with anger. Every man in the room cringed and every woman nodded in solidarity.

"So true," Goldie added.

"I do not have PMS!" My adamant protest didn't matter; the visual had been made.

McCade held up a hand and fixed his dark gaze on me. "Look, I don't care if you were possessed by demons from hell, which I guess is the same as PMS. All I know is that I'm now on vacation for a week. Have fun in *Thailand*." He tapped his brow in a little salute and walked out the door, Aunt Velma, Goldie and I all ogling his tight butt as he did so. If he was being such an ass, I might as well enjoy the view.

"Well, he can pull me over and frisk me anytime he wants," Goldie said, fanning herself.

"No kidding. I might want to get a hold of his service weapon," Aunt Velma added. "Sorry, Carl. I like your piece, too." She waggled her eyebrows.

Okay, it was now officially a little creepy lusting after the same man as Aunt Velma. "Miss Goldie, that man is a complete—"

"Now, now, it's all over," Carl cut in, obviously trying to smooth things over. "Go see if you can make another flight." He winked at Aunt Velma.

I took a deep breath. "There aren't any more flights to get there in time. The Ubon Ratchathani Candle Festival is only for two days, and it'll be almost finished before I even land."

"Did you say something about udon noodles because I sure am hungry," Aunt Velma replied, rubbing her stomach. "I had to rush out of the hospital to come to the station when Carl called, and I didn't get my soft serve in the cafeteria. I love a good swirl cone." Aunt Velma had retired ten years ago from her law practice, selling the firm to someone a few years ahead of me in high school. Since then, she'd puttered around town sticking her finger in all sorts of pies. Her latest, volunteering at the hospital.

"I didn't say udon. I said *Ubon*."

"Mmm, I could eat," Goldie added. "I love that new noodle place on Willson. Maybe they have some of those udon noodles you're talking about. It's just a block from the store. Let's go." Goldie hoisted her large handbag higher on her shoulder. The giraffe print was bold enough that she would be in danger of being shot by a hunter if she got out of town a few miles.

No one understood. I was in a parallel universe full of people who were off in their own little worlds. In other words, everyone was crazy. Even the über hot detective. I glanced at Carl who just shrugged and said, "I could eat."

I shrugged back, recognizing when it was just time to shut up and stuff my face. "Yeah, so could I," I replied grumpily.

CHAPTER 3

*C*arl dropped me and Aunt Velma off at the house, and had clearly stated he'd be stopping by later. He didn't need to add more onto that sentence for me to feel nauseated.

"That was a great lunch. We don't eat those fancy oriental noodles very often."

"Asian. They're Asian," I replied, dropping down on the couch in a food coma. I'd eaten enough pasta that I was thankful for the stretch factor of my yoga pants. It seemed being tased didn't impact my ability to eat. "Oriental is reserved these days for rugs."

Aunt Velma thought about that for a moment, then nodded, her lips pursed. "Sure. Makes sense." She tossed her handbag onto the armchair by the door. Her purse was the size of Rhode Island and always had anything anyone needed, at any time. It was like a Mary Poppins bag. If she reached in far enough, she'd pull out a freestanding lamp. "I'm glad you remembered to text Mike about your car."

Mike Ozstranski was Violet's boyfriend. They'd hit it off

in high school but had rekindled their relationship earlier in the summer in Alaska. There was a story there, but they hadn't really come up for air from fooling around to share it. He was a podiatrist but was away at a conference the past week and I figured I was lucky to have caught her with her clothes on. I'd arranged with Mike to leave my car at the airport for him to pick up when he came back, which would be in a few hours. I was supposed to be in Chicago by now, so it would have been a good trade.

"Yeah, he texted back saying he probably wouldn't have fit in the car anyway. Violet's going to get him."

Mike looked way more like Aunt Velma than I did. He was huge. A big, big guy with red hair. His was a natural ginger, which was pretty darn hot, while Aunt Velma was a natural Revlon Hot As Sin since I was in seventh grade. Mike driving the Rabbit would have been like watching a clown ride in one of those little circus cars, but he was a good guy and had been willing to wedge himself in for me.

The house phone rang. It was one of those old models that was attached to the wall with a long curly cord that let you only reach so far. No caller ID, no call waiting. It had been the same number for thirty years. Some things never changed. "Velma Dinkweiler speaking."

I rolled my eyes at her formality.

"Well, hello, Carl. What?" Aunt Velma flicked a glance at me, then turned her head away and covered the phone's mouthpiece. "No, I don't have whipped cream, but I have ice cream... What? You're bringing it. Why...oh..."

She had no volume control so I heard every word. I think I vomited a little of my lunch in my mouth when she actually giggled.

"Can I talk to him please?" I asked, holding my arm out.

"Of course, but he's not bringing ice cream later. Just—"

"Yes, just whipped cream and I really, really don't want any."

One eyebrow went up at my snippy tone, then she handed me the phone, the long cord almost straight as it stretched out. "Hey, Carl, I forgot to ask you something."

"What's up?" he asked.

"Now that my brain's a little clearer, can you please tell me how *that guy* pulled me over when he was in his own car? You don't put radar guns in personal vehicles, do you?" There was silence on the other end of the line. "Carl?"

"Well, Daph, no. No, they don't."

"Then how—"

"He just said you were going crazy fast—his words, not mine—and felt he had to pull you over. Figured once the cruiser got there, they could issue a warning."

I jumped up from the couch, paced the space in the living room I could reach with the phone cord. "You're telling me he just pulled me over on a whim?"

In my mind, I could see Carl scratching his chin, stalling. He'd been around enough to know when a few words could make a woman steaming mad.

"He wasn't even working." He sighed, probably realizing I'd wheedle it out of him anyway. "He started his vacation last night."

"He wasn't even working?" I repeated. Loudly.

"Who wasn't working?" Aunt Velma asked.

I looked at Aunt Velma, my eyes narrowed. She'd gotten a diet soda from the fridge. "Get me one of those. And guess what? That detective wasn't even on shift when he pulled me over."

Aunt Velma's mouth fell open, then pinched into a thin line. "Well, I never." She shook her head back and forth, earrings swinging, as she went back into the kitchen. I heard the fridge door open, slam shut.

"He had his gun and badge on his belt," I remembered. She handed me a soda and I braced the phone between my cheek and shoulder as I popped the top.

"He was making a stop and didn't know what to expect," Carl said.

"That's for sure," I mumbled.

"When you went all crazy on him, he didn't want to shoot you, that's why he used the taser. Even though you punched him in the nose."

I took a big swig of my soda to cool down and to keep my mouth shut for a few extra seconds.

"I didn't go all...listen, Carl, never mind. It's over. I don't have to see that guy again so let's just forget about it."

Another pause. "Really?"

I wasn't so sure what would happen if I saw Officer McHottie again, but it wasn't Carl's problem. Besides, I had to listen to the guy have sex with my aunt—Carl, not McHottie—so I needed to save something in reserve for when I needed to really yell at him. Say, later tonight.

"Really." I sighed.

"Well, all right then." He sounded relieved. "I'm going to have a patrol car drop me off and get your Rabbit and I'll bring it by later. It's the least I can do, considering."

Aunt Velma had bought the red Rabbit for me when I'd come home from boarding school the summer after I turned sixteen. It had been old and a clunker then, but I'd loved it right from the start. It had been my little piece of independence and it still was. Even though I wasn't in town often, Aunt Velma kept up with the maintenance and had it waiting for me.

"Thanks, Carl."

I glanced at Aunt Velma who was leaning against the doorway listening to the one-sided conversation. "Do you want to talk to him?'

"Just tell him not to forget the whipped cream. Oh, and tell him I've got the cherries."

That, I doubted. She hadn't had her cherry since 1971.

"Did you hear that, Carl, because I'm not repeating it."

"Gotcha." He hung up.

I untangled myself from the cord and hung the phone back up.

"What are you going to do now?" Aunt Velma asked, finished with her soda and now sifting through the mail. "Hey, I might have won a million dollars!" She held up the envelope with a sarcastic twist to her mouth, then tossed the lot into the recycling bin in the corner of the kitchen.

I sighed. "I missed the candle festival, so I've got to figure out what I'm going to do for the next assignment."

Aunt Velma perked up. "Hey. You don't have to go all the way to Thailand for candles. We can just go to the candle store at the mall. I love that pumpkin spice one, but that's seasonal and they don't always carry it."

Yeah, no. "This isn't exactly the same thing."

"Well, it was worth a try," she said, forlorn. "Don't you have another assignment lined up?"

I took another sip of soda. "Not until the end of August."

"Hmm."

That little sound was fairly innocuous coming from most people, but when Aunt Velma hmm'd, I got worried. I had good reason. The list of things that had happened to me after a hmm included getting our legs waxed because of a two-for-one coupon that came in those coupon packs in the mail, getting matching cornrows in our hair for the fifth grade International Day festival at school and building an outdoor chicken coop so we could have our own eggs. The worst was when she'd set me up on a blind double date with Hank Gilwater...and his father. When Hank and I had to watch his dad and Aunt Velma make out at the movies, then get kicked out for it, it had solidified that boarding school would be a good place for me.

Aunt Velma and I always got along, but she was a free spirit and raised me to be independent, just like she was. She'd been married back in the sixties long enough to be saddled with the last name of Dinkweiler, and that had been that for legal unions. Since then, she'd had more non-legal unions than I could remember, including Mr. Gilwater. So when I'd said I wanted to go away to boarding school, Aunt Velma understood I needed to spread my wings—her words, not mine.

Since I was stuck in Bozeman for the next few weeks—LA was most definitely out—and Aunt Velma said hmm, I was petrified. The problem was, I was too tired and too frazzled, literally, to run for the hills. Besides, my car was still sitting on the side of the Frontage Road, and the only way I was getting it back was by my aunt's boyfriend who would also be bringing whipped cream and it wasn't for dessert. Hours later, when Carl showed up with my car and a bag from Safeway, I grabbed the keys from him and left.

Something about the McHottie *incident* was bothering me. Okay, a lot about it bothered me, but one thing was still unclear. I found a spot right in front of Goldilocks and went in searching for an answer. For a Tuesday night, it was quiet, only a few patrons browsing. Veronica and Goldie were both behind the counter.

"I need every movie with Silky Tangles in it."

Veronica angled down her chin and just stared, eyes wide.

"Silky Tangles?" Goldie asked, then tapped her chin. "Well, there's *Tailed by The Police* and *Nailed in Jail.*" She went over to the wall of DVD cases, pulled those two down, then a few more. "There's also *Stuffed and Cuffed* and *Strip Searched.*"

The theme of these films did not surprise me in the least. Of course, McHottie had watched them all.

She returned to the counter and handed me a stack. Unfortunately, the covers only showed barely discreet naked bodies in interesting poses that involved all kinds of law enforcement paraphernalia. Handcuffs, I could imagine, but a billy club was a mystery to me and really, I didn't want to know.

If McHottie thought I was one of these women, I'd have to reconsider my opinion of the man. He thought I looked like them? I had nice C cups, but they weren't personal flotation devices like these ladies had.

"Crap."

"Why on earth do you want these?" Veronica asked. "I never took you for a porn flick kind of gal."

Goldie was standing there quietly, waiting to hear this answer. She knew it was going to be good. I'd never come into the store seeking anything before—I knew better—so jumping right into heavy duty porn was probably a surprise, even for her.

"That...*detective*...who pulled me over thought I was Silky Tangles."

They both looked me up and down. I'd showered and changed into a pair of cut off jean shorts and a white tank top.

Goldie tilted her head from side to side. "She's got good breasts."

"Long legs," Veronica added.

"Her hair's the right color."

"Turn around," Veronica asked.

"What?" I asked, frowning. "No way. You do not need to see my butt to know I'm not her."

Goldie grabbed a case from the pile. "Here, let's check it out."

On the side of the counter, she had a small TV with a DVD player built in. It was turned off, but once she loaded it up and got past the menu, the beginning of *Stuffed and Cuffed* came up. The volume was set pretty loud and some interesting intro music that sounded very similar to the *CHiPs* TV show theme blared. Soon enough, a police officer knocked on a scantily clad woman's door and was putting her under arrest. The patrons who'd been browsing came over to join us as well as a couple who'd just come through the door. We were all crowded around the little TV watching.

Turned out, there wasn't just one underdressed woman, but two. The second came out of the bathroom in a towel, her skin slick and wet from a shower. Her hair was styled like a beauty pageant queen and she had on perfect makeup, so the shower was somewhat of a stretch. But the three men in our little group didn't seem to care.

"Hey, that's you!" one of the men said, pointing at me.

All heads swiveled to me, looked me over, then back at the TV. Yup, there was no doubt that the shower woman, now naked, was Silky Tangles. "Holy shit," I whispered.

Veronica's mouth was hanging open. "Holy shit is right, Daph. She does look just like you."

"Can you tell me where you got your implants?" the woman who'd just come in with her boyfriend asked.

"Um," I replied. My breasts were all natural and were way smaller than the triple Ds Silky had on screen. The movie quickly shifted from interrogation to strip search. There was quite a bit of probing and repeated focus on all orifices for secret stashes of drugs or weapons. It was like watching a car crash—no one could look away. I was partially repulsed and partially intrigued. Silky Tangles really did look like me. Of course, I didn't have the thighs or the moves like she did, nor did I have the sucking power of a Hoover vacuum. She'd

clearly been in the business for a while or had been a very
early bloomer.

"Can I have your autograph?" another guy asked, his eyes
glazed with lust. Everyone started crowding around,
bombarding me with questions.

"Doesn't your mouth get tired?"

"How does the guy keep it up for so long?"

"Are you faking or is the guy really that good?"

"You don't look as big on screen, so I guess TV does add
fifteen pounds. But for you it was all in the boobs. Pretty
strange."

"What kind of lipstick is that? It doesn't even come
off...and you sure tried."

"Will you go out with me?"

My back was pressed against the glass counter and I had
my hands up. Someone placed a permanent marker in my
hand and I'd grabbed it automatically.

"Okay folks, one at a time. Silky Tangles will sign autographs, then you've got to give her some room," Goldie
announced. "Here." She gave me some scrap paper.

Five minutes later, the store was empty. Goldie had sold
two Silky Tangles videos to the guys, a set of handcuffs for
the couple and I was assured a date anytime with a guy
named Bob.

"Holy shit," I said again, stunned.

"Is there something you're not telling us, sweetheart?"

Goldie looked at me over the tops of her reading glasses
fastened to a rhinestone encrusted chain that hung about
her neck.

"What? You think I'm her?" I pointed to the TV.

"If you had your hair styled and double D implants,"
Goldie said

"You do spend a lot of time out of town," Veronica
added.

"When I envisioned having a secret life, it was as Wonder Woman, not a porn star," I countered.

"Well, you have to hand it to Miss Silky. She gives her all. And I mean literally," Veronica replied, shaking her head.

The bell over the door dinged and Jack Reid walked in. He was Veronica's lawyer boyfriend. Although he only had eyes for Veronica, I didn't mind staring at him, nor did any other woman in town under the age of ninety. He was that good looking.

"Hey, Jack," Goldie called out, putting the DVDs back on the shelf.

"Have you ever heard of Silky Tangles?" Veronica asked.

Jack stopped in his tracks halfway to the counter. "Oh crap, this is one of those questions, isn't it? Hey, Daphne."

I gave him a little head nod but really wanted to hear what he had to say.

Veronica just raised her eyebrows.

"Fine." He sighed. "I'm doomed here. If you're talking about Silky Tangles, the porn star, then I've never heard of her."

"Really?" Veronica grinned and came around the counter to wrap her arms around her man.

"I'm a lawyer. I plead the fifth."

"Smart." She kissed him. "Very smart."

"What do you want me to say, that she's really Daphne?"

"How did you know?" Goldie asked in complete surprise, one hand covering the word SASSY on her chest.

"Goldie," I replied dryly. "Don't encourage him."

Jack grinned at me. "I've known since Ty's bachelor party."

Ty Strickland was Goldie's daughter-in-law Jane's fiancé. Jane had been married to Goldie's son until he died about five years ago from some kind of aneurysm or something. They'd been getting divorced at the time so Jane wasn't overly heartbroken, although it must be hard for Goldie to lose her only child. Jane helped Goldie run the store and Ty was a Bozeman firefighter. They were getting married in September.

"Oh my god, you guys watched porn and thought it was me? Thailand isn't far enough away," I groaned, mortified.

"You're really good with your mouth. How do you keep the lipstick on?" he asked. I could tell by the way he was trying not to smile that he was kidding.

Veronica smacked him on the arm. "Jack Reid, how could you?"

Jack looked down at Veronica, ran his knuckles over her cheek. "I watched the movie, then came home to you, babe. Remember? That was the night we did that thing with the ties since we didn't have any handcuffs. I remember because you called out—"

Veronica covered his mouth with her hand. "Don't you dare," she hissed.

He nipped at her fingers then kissed her again, this time with a whole lot of tongue. "Goldie, if you're quiet for the night, I've got some plans for Veronica."

Goldie just shook her head and laughed, waved her hand toward the door. "Go. Just go. Daphne can stay and help."

I whipped my head around to Goldie. Stay and help?

The couple bolted for the door before I could even argue. Realizing I'd been well and truly caught, I exhaled and joined Goldie behind the counter.

"Here. Sort these. Somehow the strawberry flavored condoms got mixed in with the mint ones."

She handed me two boxes with individually wrapped condoms to sort. At least I wouldn't be bored. The store was one big room styled to replicate a Las Vegas casino, circa 1960. There was an abundance of gold and lots of crazy carpet.

"So, sweetheart, is there something you want to tell me?" She sat on a stool by the cash register giving me room to spread out my task on the glass counter. I didn't look up from my sorting.

"About what exactly? That I missed my assignment in Thailand or that I was tased by Officer Hot Pants or that my aunt is having sex with Carl and a can of whipped cream or that people think I'm Silky Tangles?"

"Officer Hot Pants?" Goldie got a dreamy expression. "Yeah, that name fits him, and so did those jeans today. I haven't seen him in a long time, and he sure looks fine. You could have your way with him, especially if you tell him you really are Silky Tangles."

"Goldie, I don't want to be with a guy because he thinks I'm a porn star. He'd learn the truth when he got me naked— did you see that woman's butt? Besides, I can definitely say my repertoire in the bedroom does not include the things in that movie."

"If you watch them, you can pick up some pointers."

I just turned my head to look at her.

"Right. Okay then." She held up her hands. "So you're not a porn star, and I can't help you with Officer Hot Pants. I'm well aware of Velma and Carl, but certainly missed the whipped cream part. I'm sure if you go home, you won't. I'm all for fun in the bedroom, but seeing your aunt in action isn't good. How about this? I've got my old camper parked in front of my house because I'm selling it. You can stay in it tonight. It's all cleaned up and ready to go."

Goldie's camper or a live porno starring Aunt Velma. The decision wasn't tough. "Great, thanks, Goldie."

A camper in Montana was like a boat in Florida. So many people had them and it wasn't strange to see one in a driveway or in front of a house, especially this time of year. Big Sky country was for exploring and playing and a camper was the way to go. It was better than a tent because you didn't have to worry about bears.

"Just don't use the toilet. It's all primed and ready to go for the new owners."

"Sure, no problem." I'd rather hold it in than stay at home.

Goldie clicked her manicured nails on the counter. "As for your assignment, hmm."

Oh man. A hmm from Goldie? This wasn't good.

CHAPTER 4

$\mathcal{N}$othing else exciting happened before closing. Thankfully. No one else recognized me, for which I was relieved. More worrisome, however, was that Goldie had been surprisingly quiet. She was *never* quiet. I pulled my Rabbit into the driveway and stared at the dark house I'd lived in since I was five. It was built early in the 1900s on the north side of Main when the city started to grow after the gold rush tapered off and other industry moved in. It was considered a bungalow with a combination of brick and wood painted white. The windows were big and original, which meant lots of light but plenty of drafts in the winter. Aunt Velma had bought it after her divorce and when my parents dumped me with her, she converted the attic into a bedroom for me. The roof slanted on both sides so it was cozy and great for a short person. As I grew, I'd had to watch my head as the ceiling quickly became the walls. Aunt Velma was an avid gardener and people drove or walked by to see the yard, especially this time of year when it was in all its glory.

I tiptoed inside with a large amount of dread about what I

might see or hear. I dashed up the narrow stairs off the kitchen, found a change of clothes and my old Scooby Doo sleeping bag, and made it back to the car without hearing anything that would scar me for life.

Goldie's house was about ten blocks away on the other side of Main. Sure enough, there was Goldie's old camper. Old was an optimal word. It was very vintage, so vintage I thought I'd seen it on an episode of *The Brady Bunch*. Perhaps I was confusing it with *Buck Rogers*. It was a camper and car built in one, meaning it didn't need to be towed. It was metallic with a red stripe down the side. It reminded me of a great big steel pickle heading for outer space. I ducked my head and went in the side door and flipped on the lights. I wasn't driving it, so I didn't need a key and not much bad stuff happened in Bozeman. It was almost an unwritten code that you didn't mess with another person's camper.

In front of me was a tiny kitchen counter with a built-in stovetop, a mini fridge beneath and a few drawers. A toaster oven took up most of the miniscule counter space along with a coffeemaker. To the left was a bench seat with a table and another bench seat across where a kid could sleep. If I remembered correctly, the table folded down and the two seats somehow morphed into a bed. Supposedly for grown-ups, but I highly doubted that unless they were under five feet tall. In the other direction there was a recliner against one wall, clearly a Goldie modernization. Across from it were fold-down bunk beds, just like on a train; stowed during the day and lowered for sleeping. Past that was a small door which had to be the bathroom, then another door that led to a bedroom. Literally, a bed with a door for privacy. The pickle slept two if you were on your honeymoon and six to eight if you really liked each other. An awful lot.

I turned out the light and made my way into the back

bedroom. It was cool, only in the fifties even though it was July, so I threw on my sweatshirt and spread out my sleeping bag. I could hear the wind in the trees and nothing else. No sex. No headboard banging. Nothing. My life was a total wreck. Even though Roger and I hadn't really been together for a while, my relationship status was officially single. The first hot guy I get near and he tases me. I signed autographs for a porn star. I was homeless, bedded down in my childhood sleeping bag and spending the night in a used camper. My life needed serious work. Decisions needed to be made because I was just as aimless as I had been at fifteen. But not now. I'd had enough insanity for one day, so I called it a night.

"Hello!" Goldie trilled from the door. I sat up and rubbed my eyes trying to remember where I was. Oh yeah, the camper. The bed swayed as Goldie came inside; the stabilizers weren't down to balance the RV. "Oh good, you're up. I've figured out all of your problems," she responded almost gleefully.

The bed dipped again. "I think it's going to be perfect, and so much fun!" Aunt Velma's voice was loud in the small space.

I looked at my watch, wiped the sleep from my eyes. Hmm. Ten. The sun was bright through metal blinds covering the small window on the back wall. Goldie sat down on the edge of the bed. Aunt Velma ducked her head through the doorway and sat down as well, forcing me to curl my feet up inside my sleeping bag. Staring at them was like a shot of espresso. Goldie's hair was down in soft waves and she wore a leopard print shirt with another pair of jeggings, these in black. Aunt Velma wore a Day-Glo orange exercise shirt and striped shorts. She looked like a golfer who'd gotten lost in the eighties. With her red hair, it was an impressive combination.

"Oh?" I asked noncommittally, my voice scratchy.

"It came to me last night. I need to get this camper to Omaha to my cousin Ralph's brother's son's house. His neighbor is going to buy it."

I sniffed. "Isn't your cousin Ralph's brother also your cousin?"

Goldie pondered for a moment. "Huh, you're right. I guess I could say then that we're taking it to my cousin Ralph's nephew's house."

I was really, really sorry I asked because either way, it was still in Omaha. "Why doesn't he come here to pick it up himself?" Sounded like a long way to make Goldie go to sell her own camper.

"He was going to, but then Velma and I realized it would be a perfect writing assignment for you."

Okay, they were starting to make plans for me, so I perked up. Propping up on my elbows, I gave them the evil eye. "Me?"

They had deflector shields or something because they didn't pick up on my wary tone. "You need something to write about for that travel magazine. What better than a road trip across the American West?" Aunt Velma asked. "It's perfect! There's so much to see and people will love to read about our trip."

"*Our* trip?" I asked. This wasn't good.

Goldie nodded. "You, me and Velma. We'll pick up Esther Millhouse on the way. You need to brush your teeth." Goldie fanned her face.

I sat up, propped my back against the wall, my feet still in my sleeping bag. "You guys woke me up," I grumbled. I could feel the fur coating my teeth. "Let's keep on topic here. You want me to go on a road trip, in this camper, with you, Aunt Velma and Esther Millhouse?"

I had no idea who Esther Millhouse was, but if she was friends with Lucy and Ethel here, it wasn't going to be good. "Who is this woman?"

"She's our dearest, oldest friend."

Did Goldie mean that literally, like she was really, really old?

"Velma knows her from their time in Fargo with the Roller Dolls, but she lives here now. She's been in Billings visiting with her daughter and family but wants to go with us. So we'll pick her up there."

"Omaha is a long way. It's even in a different time zone, right?"

"I looked it up on that map program on the computer. It's only fifteen hours of driving. We can be there in two days. Imagine, we can see Mt. Rushmore and all the other great things along the way!" Aunt Velma exclaimed.

"We can see the world's largest porch swing in Nebraska, too. I love those kinds of things," Goldie added, clearly excited about the prospect of a road trip.

"I'm not so sure the magazine is going to be interested in this," I countered, considering this could be the demise of my career.

Aunt Velma frowned. "Why not?"

"Because the largest porch swing isn't what people want to read about."

"How would you know?" Goldie asked. "Besides, that candle thing in Thailand doesn't sound that interesting."

"Look, I haven't had my coffee yet. Let me at least get some caffeine in me before I make any crazy decisions."

"Fine," Aunt Velma said. "Perfectly understandable. Caffeine is a requirement for good judgment, but we have to get going."

My eyebrows went up. "Going? Now?"

"If we're going to meet Esther in Billings we do."

I shook my head. "Thanks, ladies, but I'm going to pass."

Goldie patted my leg through the Scooby Doo sleeping bag. Yes, someone got a kick out of the whole Velma and Daphne thing when I was in fourth grade and got it for me for my birthday. "Listen, sweetheart. There's a little problem."

Oh crap. When Goldie said there was a little problem, it meant the sky was falling.

"Someone posted on Facebook that Silky Tangles was at the store last night and handed out autographs. It even went out on Twitter."

"It's a small town. No one reads that stuff," I countered.

Goldie just gave me a look that screamed *Seriously?* "I'll have you know I have over twelve thousand followers on Twitter and have my own hashtag. When I searched last, my hashtag and Silky's hashtag were both going viral."

I had no idea Goldie knew what viral meant other than getting sick; it was important never to underestimate her.

"Since it's a small town, people are going to be hounding you," she added.

I wasn't so sure about that, but I kept it to myself. I was not popular, in no way had triple Ds and definitely was not that limber. I was *not* Silky Tangles in any way.

"We'll split up the tasks for the trip," Goldie continued. "I'll get the food, because you know I'll get the good junk food, unlike Velma."

True, Aunt Velma would get some kind of twigs and berries and health crap and call it a snack. Besides diet soda, she was a health food freak. Aunt Velma lifted her chin and sniffed. "In the spirit of friendship and a lengthy road trip, I will agree to that."

Goldie just shook her head and rolled her eyes. "Velma's going to get packed and coordinate with Esther Millhouse.

You"—Goldie pointed to me—"need to take the camper to get gas and while you're at the convenience store, pick up a couple bags of ice."

I climbed out my sleeping bag and nudged the ladies aside so I could get out of the bedroom. "Coffee," I said, tucking my hair behind my ear. "Then I'll go and fill the RV for you, but I'm not committing to anything until I've had caffeine." I grabbed my keys and left the ladies sitting there.

* * *

AN HOUR LATER, I stood at a pump at the convenience store on East Main filling the old RV with gas. I'd been able to head home to get my coffee, brush my teeth and take a shower. I'd thrown on an old t-shirt, shorts and flip flops and put my wet hair up into a sloppy bun. No way was I going with the ladies on this trip. It was one of those kamikaze missions where you knew going in you wouldn't come out alive. But if I helped them gas up the old RV and got the ice they needed, the faster they'd be off and out of my hair. Then I could be back in my old bedroom once again, without the sex noises coming through the walls.

The auto shut off clicked after about four million gallons and I put the gas nozzle back on the pump. I climbed into the pickle, cranked the engine and put it in gear. Of course, a big SUV with out-of-state tags pulled up and parked, blocking me. A woman hopped out and grabbed a little girl from the back and made a mad dash into the building. Ah, emergency pee break. Unfortunately, the RV was too big to wedge between the pumps and the back of the SUV. I looked in the side view mirrors. It was all clear, so I could just back up far enough past the pumps to turn out. Putting the RV in Reverse, I slowly backed up.

No big deal. I could drive the space pickle. It wasn't hard.

Sure, it didn't have a rearview mirror, but it had great side ones. It was taller than a car and definitely longer, but I was a great driver, even going ninety. I just had to be sure to make wide turns. Piece of—

Crunch.

The RV shook and a horrible metal on metal sound had me slamming on the brakes, even though I was only going less than five miles an hour. Somehow the back-left corner seemed to be higher than before. I yanked the gear shift up into Park and hopped out, working my way around to the back to see what I'd hit.

Oh shit. A beautiful motorcycle was on its side, the front wheel caught beneath the back tire of the RV. The bike was all gleaming chrome pipes and wide handlebars with a black leather seat. A shiny turquoise gas tank sparkled and shimmered like a bowling ball. This wasn't a dirt bike and this definitely wasn't a moped. This screamed testosterone-laden, red-blooded, all-American male. I ducked down, making sure I hadn't crushed the red-blooded male like the Wicked Witch of the East. Fortunately, no dead body, no testosterone dripping all over the ground. My stomach dropped out of my throat, but my adrenaline still hummed through my veins.

"Hey!" a guy shouted, running toward me, holding a black helmet in one hand. "What the fuck?"

I looked up from my crouch and, low and behold, there was Officer McHottie. I stood and his anger morphed into surprise.

"You! Are you kidding me? Jesus, you ran over my bike!" He ran his hand over his hair, his jaw clenched tight. "Pull forward and get that...that space ship off the front tire."

His words snapped me out of my trance. I was freaked out that I might have killed someone, then relieved that I hadn't, then wished that I had all within about thirty seconds. Since I had no idea what to say and I was completely in the wrong, I hopped in the RV and slowly eased it forward until I felt the back end even out.

Returning to the rear, we were able to see the damage. McHottie knelt down in front of the motorcycle acting like I'd run over his dog. He looked sad, dejected and royally pissed. We'd drawn a crowd. All of the men were practically crying at the damage I'd caused. I didn't know much about motorcycles—I knew nothing about them actually—but I could tell by the way people were reacting that I might have run over the two-wheeled version of a Rolls Royce.

"Hey, you're Silky Tangles," a middle-aged guy said, pointing at me.

The woman standing next to him frowned. "Who's Silky Tangles?"

"She's...oh shit," he muttered, clearly caught knowing who a porn star was.

"Yeah, it is her. I'd recognize that body anywhere." This came from a kid in his early twenties. He was smiling at me in a way a lounge lizard scoped out women at a singles bar.

McHottie gave me the look that screamed *See?*

I ignored the porn-loving men and knelt down across from McHottie, the bike between us. Even with the strong gas fumes, I could pick up his clean, spicy scent. I bit my lip, afraid to ask. "Will...will it still ride?" I asked cautiously.

His eyes narrowed and his jaw clenched tight. It probably wasn't the right thing to say. He pointed to the front wheel, which was all mangled and bent. "The tire's popped, the rim's dented and the fork's bent."

Yeah, it wasn't going anywhere anytime soon. I felt like crap. If someone hit the Rabbit, I'd be pretty mad, too. And my Rabbit was nowhere near as nice as this motorcycle. "I'm sorry. Really, I didn't see it there."

"You are a menace to society," he growled. "Did you even look?"

He was mad, but still. I felt insulted. "Of course I looked, but it was in the blind spot." He kept staring at me as if he wanted to lunge across the dead bike and strangle me. "You don't have your Taser, do you?" I asked warily.

"Lady, what I want to do to you doesn't involve a Taser," he replied, a vein pulsing at his temple.

My body heated at those words, even though I was sure he didn't mean anything carnal. It was hard to keep my thoughts from going that way when his jeans were stretched taut over very muscular thighs and his black leather jacket was...wow. He hadn't shaved yet and his dark stubble made him look a little dangerous. Okay, a lot dangerous. I could only imagine what he looked like riding that bike. Thankfully, he wasn't wearing his gun, or at least I couldn't see it, and I didn't know where he'd hide it.

"Dude, your bike got totaled by Silky Tangles. Cool. I know how I'd make her pay for damages," the college kid's friend told McHottie.

McHottie's jaw clenched...again, and he stood to his full height, much taller and broader than the college kid. This was the look of doom he'd given me yesterday on the side of the road right before he tased me. Obviously, it hadn't scared me since he'd had to fry my brain cells, but the college kid looked really freaked out. He practically peed his pants and slinked off to his car with his buddy and left. Others backed away slowly and went about their day.

"I'll pay for the damages." I stood and held up my hands in surrender. "Let's just get it to a mechanic and it will be as good as new."

He just shook his head as if I were an idiot. "You can't just take this bike to a mechanic. It needs to go to Bob, a guy who fixes Harley's. But he's in Sturgis. I'd be there too in about eight hours if you hadn't backed into the bike." He placed his hands on his hips. His narrow hips that looked very nice with a pair of low-slung jeans about them.

Sturgis, South Dakota, hosted an annual motorcycle rally, famous among the motorcycle crowd. I knew nothing about motorcycles and I'd even heard of it. Bikers migrated there like monarch butterflies year after year for a week of fun. I'd never been, so I had no idea what actually happened, but most likely it included a lot of leather and definitely involved a crap load of motorcycles. A bike was pretty much a requirement. And, it seemed, it was happening now. Because of me, without McHottie.

I licked my lips nervously. "I'm really sorry." I felt terrible. I didn't have to like the guy to feel bad that his plans had been messed up. My phone rang. I pulled it from my pocket. Goldie.

"Where are you? We're at the house waiting," she said.

"Oh, um. I ran into a little trouble at the gas station." I nibbled on my lip and glanced at McHottie. He rolled his eyes at my pun. Of course, I hadn't meant it. *Right.*

"Where are you?"

"On East Main."

"We'll be there in five minutes." Goldie clicked off before I could tell her not to come, but she lived just down the street and wouldn't steer clear of trouble if it was about to run her over. Maybe when Goldie and Aunt Velma showed up, *I* wouldn't look quite as crazy. It was a long five minutes, McHottie getting on his cell and talking to someone, gesturing with his hands in ways that indicated several different options for my demise. For once, I was thankful to see Goldie's car squeal into the lot practically on two wheels. The windows were rolled down and the latest Coldplay song blasted. She and Aunt Velma hopped out and assessed the situation, hands on hips.

"Hey, we know you," Aunt Velma said. "You're Officer McHottie."

Oh my god. I should just reach into the guy's jacket pocket, pull out his gun and kill myself. It would be less painful than the mortification of this moment.

"McHottie?" He shut his eyes and just shook his head. Yup, at least now he knew crazy was hereditary. He sighed. "Yeah, I know you, too."

Clearly yesterday's debacle wasn't forgotten by anyone.

Goldie shouldered her way into the group and looked down at the motorcycle. "I'll get Bob on the horn and he'll fix that right up."

McHottie glanced at Goldie. "You know Bob?"

Goldie looked surprised. "Sure. Everyone knows Bob."

I didn't know Bob.

"He's my brother-in-law's nephew on his wife's side's neighbor," Goldie explained.

McHottie froze, processed. And now I knew why I didn't know Bob.

"I've got him on speed dial." She whipped out her cell and dialed him right up. "Hey, Bob, it's Goldie. No, that movie hasn't come in yet. You're first on the waiting list." She listened. "Yes, I know it's got Silky Tangles in it."

I rolled my eyes.

"Look, I need a new front wheel for a Harley Softtail Fat Boy pronto. It looks like"—she leaned in toward the bike to get a better look—"a new front fork, too." She listened. "Uh huh, I see. You're there now, huh? 'Til when? Right."

We all stared at her, including McHottie, stunned she could name a Harley model just by looking at it. She never ceased to amaze.

"Yes, it's JT's bike. Is that so?" She continued her conversation with the infamous Bob, but turned to look at McHottie.

"You arranged that for JT? Are you sure that's a good idea? Oh, right, that makes sense. He is on vacation."

Goldie grinned and looked at JT—I couldn't call him McHottie anymore since I knew his real name—in a new way I couldn't interpret. Bob said something that piqued Goldie's curiosity, and it had to do with JT. And it had to have a story. Goldie loved a good story.

"All right. That's not a bad idea." She nodded her head. "Give me a few minutes and I'll get back to you. Thanks, Bob." Goldie hung up, waggled her eyebrows. "So, JT, I guess you really want to get to Sturgis?"

JT just looked at Goldie for a moment, then muttered a bad word under his breath. "He told you?"

She nodded slowly. "It's been a long time since I've seen you, but you should remember, everyone tells me *everything*."

Aunt Velma and I looked between the two, completely clueless. It was as if they spoke in a foreign language.

"Bob's in Sturgis for the rally like JT said," Goldie added.

"Yeah, that's the problem," JT replied, pointing down at the broken bike.

"We're actually headed to Omaha in that." Goldie pointed at the pickle, which now that my heart rate had returned to normal, I saw had a nice big dent in the back bumper and undercarriage. Great. Hopefully Goldie wouldn't notice it since she was selling it. "I've got a trailer in storage we can put your bike on and take it...and you, to Sturgis. It's on the way. It's the least we can do. Bob said if we call him when we get there, he can arrange to get the bike fixed."

JT looked surprised. "Really?"

"Really. You don't believe me?" Goldie countered archly.

He held up a hand in front of him. "No, ma'am. I believe you." He scratched the back of his neck, clearly unsure of what to say. "It's just that it's Sturgis and there are going to be thousands of Harleys. I figure Bob will be too busy having fun to take on a fix while he's there."

Goldie cracked her knuckles. "That's most likely true, but people seem to just want to help me."

"Is it perhaps because you know if someone likes to watch girl on girl porn or purchased the triple donger for an anniversary present?" Aunt Velma clarified. "Or in Bob's case, the new movie starring Silky Tangles?" She turned her gaze to me.

I just looked at her with my *What?* stare.

Goldie shrugged.

"Like you said, it's been a long time since I've been in your store," JT told Goldie, his face hard and lacking emotion. "You don't have anything on me that isn't ancient history."

Goldie winked slyly. "I do now."

JT's cheeks flushed crimson and he pursed his lips into a tight line.

"So, need that ride to Sturgis?"

CHAPTER 5

*J*t only took an hour to get the broken bike up on a flatbed trailer and the whole thing hooked up to the back of the RV. The two guys who brought it most likely had some weird sexual fetishes that they were afraid Goldie would let slip. Little did they know that Goldie never told. Ever. Clearly not knowing that, they had the bike secured quickly and efficiently. They paused and offered their condolences to JT before they drove off. I stayed as far away from the man as possible.

"I need to pack."

"You both do," Goldie cut in. She tossed me her keys, but I wasn't ready, so I fumbled for them like a woman scrambling for a tossed wedding bouquet. "Perhaps it's best if you take my car and I drive the RV."

"Good thinking," Aunt Velma added. "Let's meet back at Goldie's house in say...an hour?"

Goldie nodded and we all looked to JT. He was staring forlornly at his bike. "One hour. I can't believe I'm saying this"—he sighed heavily—"but I'll ride with Goldie. You should have your license revoked." He pointed at me like

Uncle Sam on those recruiting posters then walked over to the passenger door of the pickle. Climbing in, he slammed the door hard enough to rock the RV from side to side.

"Those are some mighty fine buns of steel," Aunt Velma whispered. Very loudly.

A woman with a Disneyland t-shirt and Day-Glo jog shorts had paused with her super-sized slushy and enjoyed the view—the back half of JT—with us. "Mmm mmm. They sure make them fine up here in Montana."

Yes, ma'am, they sure did.

* * *

WE PULLED into Goldie's driveway right on schedule. Aunt Velma was a stickler for punctuality, so I couldn't be sure I'd included everything I needed for a road trip across the American West. My bag had been packed, ready for Thailand, so I swapped out a few things for extreme heat and humidity with a little lightweight fleece.

JT was leaning over his bike, adjusting the yellow ratchet straps that held it down. I didn't get anywhere near him. Not that I was avoiding the man, which I was, but because if something else happened to the bike, it wasn't going to be my fault. Didn't mean I couldn't stare at his butt from a distance.

"All ready!" Goldie pranced out of her house, the screen door slapping behind her. She hadn't changed but added square sunglasses that were so dark I couldn't see her eyes and so big she wouldn't need sunscreen on her face. "I'm so excited. At first, I thought this was going to be a dull trip, but it's shaped up into something fun!"

I'd never seen Goldie so perky before. It was as if she'd had three cups of coffee and an energy drink since we saw her an hour ago. Calm Goldie was frightening enough. I had no idea what she'd come up with if her mind moved any faster.

"I'm ready GG," a voice called from inside. "I went pee just like you said. And here's my pee bottle!"

A boy of about seven or eight came barreling out Goldie's front door. In one hand he had an empty soda bottle, clearly his emergency pee container, and in the other a—what the hell was that?

"Hi, Aunt Velma," he cried, running over to give her legs a hug. He wasn't a small child, but Velma was like Hagrid from *Harry Potter* in comparison. Getting a closer look, I saw that in his hand was a ceramic garden gnome. Little red jacket, pointy blue hat, big cheeky grin. Why he carried it, I had no idea.

"Great, Zach, hop on in and find a spot with a seatbelt and buckle up."

For the first time, I think JT and I had similar expressions. Complete confusion. I leaned my head toward Aunt Velma. "Um, why is that kid going with us?" I whispered.

"That's Zach, Goldie's grandson. He's got a friend in Billings and we're going to take him over there and leave him. His mom, you know Jane West, will get him tomorrow. I told them to go to the Olive Garden. I love that restaurant. All you can eat breadsticks and salad. Pity Billings has the closest one."

I tried to keep up, but I had to admit, I got hungry when she mentioned breadsticks. "So two hours with a kid?" I asked. I knew Jane, sort of. The last time I'd seen Zach he was toddling around, so it had definitely been awhile.

I had nothing against this kid specifically, but I wasn't good with them in general. My little kid days with my parents were just blurry images in my head and Aunt Velma had tried her best, but even though I had been one didn't mean I could be responsible enough for raising one without causing the poor kid serious mental issues.

Velma turned to look at me, disapproval on her face. "Daphne Lane. You don't like kids?"

"I do." Sort of. "Don't they always ask, *Are we there yet* over and over?"

Aunt Velma pursed her lips. "Well, that's true. But it's only two hours."

Right, only two hours. Gilligan and his crew went out for three-hour tour and never came back.

"Saddle up!" Goldie called, hopping into the RV.

JT hadn't said a word, hadn't gotten near us. I had a feeling he wanted to be anywhere on the planet besides riding in a metallic pickle with two borderline geriatric women, a woman he'd tased and a kid holding a garden gnome and a pee bottle. Climbing in and shutting the door behind him had to be one of the hardest things he'd ever had to do.

Even though he was a complete jerk, I sympathized because I felt just about the same way. Although, it was going to be pretty dang hard not to jump his bones with his fabulous scent filling the closed space for several hundred miles. It was possible the pheromones he pumped out would pull Goldie and Aunt Velma right out of menopause.

Goldie took the driver's seat, Aunt Velma claimed shotgun, with Zach sitting behind her in a chair I hadn't noticed before, which dropped from the wall like a jump seat for a flight attendant on an airplane. He was all buckled in safely and the three of them were gabbing away.

JT and I sat on the bench seats further back, me behind the small table, he, with his legs stretched out, across from me. "You know this is all your fault," he said bitterly.

"Me?"

"You ran over my motorcycle." He crossed his arms over his chest.

I leaned forward, bracing my forearms on the table. "You made me miss my plane. If you had just let me go, I'd be somewhere over the Pacific Ocean right now, and I wouldn't have hit your flipping motorcycle. And I wouldn't be riding in this RV either."

I had a point and by the hard set of his jaw, he knew it. "It's still your fault."

I rolled my eyes as I tucked my ear buds in, hoping to drown him out with music from my cell phone.

Once we got on the interstate, we started to make progress, but very slowly. The pickle couldn't handle the hills on the east side of town, and we had to cross Bozeman Pass to get out of the Gallatin Valley. We were going so slow even a combine passed us in the left lane.

I, of course, made no mention of this since it wouldn't help us go any faster, so I pulled out my e-reader and buried my nose behind it, pretending to enjoy a book.

"Jesus, I could walk up this hill faster," JT grumbled, loud enough I could hear it over my music.

A truer statement had never been said. Even me, who only ran when chased by an axe-wielding murderer, could have scaled the steep highway faster. It was almost impossible to be patient when my life was moving forward at twenty miles an hour.

By the time we started our descent at the top of the pass, I really had gotten into my book and only looked up when we were slowing at the end of an exit ramp.

"Why are we getting off the highway?" I called forward.

Aunt Velma glanced over her shoulder. "It's a Trekker Truck Stop. When you get a large drink, you pay once and get free refills at every one along the way."

Goldie maneuvered the RV into the large lot and parked

in a pull in/pull out spot. The place was huge—rows and rows of gas pumps, more eighteen wheelers than I could count. The large sign boasted an all-u-can-eat buffet for $4.99 and free hot showers with purchase.

"Stay with me, Zach. You two, this is our first stop, so make the most of it," Goldie added before she hopped out, her grandson dexterously jumping down behind her.

"Why can't we keep driving and just use the bathroom in back?" JT asked, angling his head in that direction.

"Goldie says she's got the tanks all filled so it would be perfect for the new owner," Aunt Velma replied before she too, exited. "Doesn't want the guy to have to empty out our waste."

I crinkled my face up.

"Then what's the point of a camper?" JT grumbled. "This is going to take forever. We're only in Livingston."

Livingston was the next town over from Bozeman, a usual twenty to thirty-minute drive away. I only shrugged, knowing nothing I could say would be helpful, then followed the herd into the building.

After taking care of business, I heard Goldie call to me from across the convenience store over the canned Karen Carpenter song blaring from the ceiling speakers. She stood by the soda machines waving a large plastic to-go cup. "What do you want? Cola? Iced Tea?"

Everyone turned to look at Goldie, who had an exceptional ability to project her voice and a complete lack of concern about what people thought of her.

"Tea," I called back. The truckers who were shopping for preservative-rich nibbles swiveled their heads back and forth between us like they were watching a tennis match.

Goldie nodded and turned back to the machines, grabbing another cup from the dispenser.

"Hey, you look mighty familiar," one man said, walking

over to me. He looked like the fourth ZZ Top. "Hey!" His face lit up in a big smile, one gold tooth bright and shiny. "You're in those cop movies. Hey, Ronald, check on this!"

Ronald, who apparently took his fashion sense from country music stars—sporting a pair of jeans, big rodeo belt buckle and a plaid button up with the sleeves hacked off—came around the aisle with the chips and pretzels. "What is it, Ralph?"

Ralph nodded at me as he held a bag of BBQ chips and started chowing down. Crumbs fell down and got lost in his beard. He pointed at me, one seasoned chip between his fingers.

Ronald swung his gaze my way and dropped his coffee, splashing the brown sludge all over the tile floor. "Holy shit. You're...I mean, you know who you are. Can I—"

"What Ronald's trying to say—he really doesn't have a stutter," Ralph cut in, "is that you're our favorite actress. Very realistic. When you put your foot behind your head in that special move you do, do you ever get stuck?"

I just stared at the men, open-mouthed.

"Can I get your autograph?" Ronald asked, completely in awe of me. "Around my belly button?"

I cringed.

"Here you go." Goldie thrust a big cup in my hand. "I got the Colonic Canon size. Hello, boys."

Ronald and Ralph nodded, but they kept their gazes pinned on me, as if afraid I might run off. Which I might if they'd just blink. "Is she your agent?"

"Agent?" Goldie wondered as she took a sip from her straw.

Ralph ran his fingers over the bottom of his beard. "I understand why you'd need to have someone with you, being famous and all. I mean...you're Silky Tangles!"

Goldie raised an eyebrow, no doubt enjoying this mix-up immensely. If I'd known any better, I'd say she planned it. I took a sip from my own colossal straw to avoid answering.

"Why don't you take a quick picture and then we'll be on our way," Goldie offered, waving her hand in a herding motion for the men to stand next to me.

Ronald didn't hesitate. He pulled his phone from his pocket and handed it to Goldie. Both men moved to stand as close to me as possible and Ronald wrapped an arm around my shoulder, his meaty hand sweaty. The pulsing flash brought me out of my stupor. I gave both men a tight smile and wriggled out of Ronald's grasp.

"Boy, look at the time." I glanced down at my watch-free wrist. "We should be moving on if we want to meet Zach's friend in Billings."

Ralph and Ronald offered their thanks and we left them staring at the small phone screen. "I'll be sure to share this on Facebook," he called out.

Great.

We got in line to pay for our drinks. "New friends?" The deep timbre of JT's voice made my nipples harden. I didn't even have to see him to get all hot and bothered. I wouldn't mind writing something around *his* belly button. Just because he was a jerk didn't mean it wouldn't be fun.

"Mmm," I replied noncommittally.

"Or are they fans? Guys who aren't just imagining what you look like beneath your clothes, but *know*?"

I spun around, ready to tell him I was *not* Silky Tangles for the umpteenth time. But when his face was right there, his dark eyes so piercing that he could practically hypnotize a woman out of her panties, I decided against it. It was the cocky grin that had me changing tactics.

I shrugged casually, moved a step forward in line. "It's important to me that I'm available to my fans."

"Available?" He took a sip of his coffee and eyed me over the brim.

"This is a truck stop, the perfect place to build my fan base." I sighed. "Besides, it's great men recognize me even without my hair styled and the fake eyelashes. Don't forget the clothes. They even recognize me *in* clothes. Just like you did before the whole taser thing."

One of his eyebrows went up, the little scar shifting into the shape of a comma. His coffee was forgotten, but he still held it up by his mouth. "So, you're saying—"

"Give me your drink, Daphne," Goldie told me, interrupting us. "Go get Zach away from that barrel of beef jerky. If he eats any of it, he'll have diarrhea for a week, especially the jalapeño flavor."

I grinned at the surprised look on JT's face and put a little extra shift in my hips on my way over to the jerky barrel, although yoga pants and an old t-shirt weren't that alluring.

We made it to Billings in a record setting pace of four hours. It was the slowest trip ever made by a motorized vehicle when the roads were dry. Lewis and Clark had made it by boat faster back in the day. Besides the break at the first truck stop outside Livingston, we hit the next one as well because everyone drank too much of their beverages. Goldie's ban on the RV's bathroom made for very slow going. There were four men waiting at the next Trekker for me, or Silky Tangles, so I signed autographs then beelined for the safety of the empty ladies' room. How the men knew I was going to be there had me stumped until they mentioned something about Facebook.

Zach was met by his friend and his friend's mother in the parking lot of a McDonalds off the highway. After a quick romp in the Playland, they were on their way. The remainder of us waited for Esther Millhouse. Aunt Velma was napping in the back bedroom, her snoring cutting through the quiet like a buzz saw in the springtime. Goldie read from her e-reader in the driver's seat, her rhinestone encrusted eyeglass holder that ran around her neck sparkling in the sunlight. JT paced outside the RV on his cell as he took a sip from another cup of coffee. If I'd drank as much caffeine as he had, I'd be up for a week. I was stuck at the miniscule dinette with my laptop trying to eke out the beginnings of a road trip article. So far, the topic was Truck Stops of the West, but it was early enough in the trip to be hopeful for more.

We were so far behind I didn't know if Esther was late or we'd missed her and she'd given up. I glanced at my watch with a sigh. Four o'clock. At the rate we were going, we wouldn't be to Sturgis until the middle of the night. Just when I was about to close up the lid on my computer and take a nap myself, a horn blared to the tune of *Dixie*. Montana was definitely a red state and folks leaned toward the conservative, but I didn't consider it a part of the South. We weren't remotely near the Mason-Dixon line, and it was more about cowboys and Indians out here than the North and South.

"There she is!" Aunt Velma called out. She ducked her head to fit through the small bedroom doorway, her red hair matted flat on one side.

I pulled down a slat in the metal shade on the window behind me. Nothing stood out of the ordinary until a woman who was about five foot nothing, had blinding white hair and wore a purple velour track suit climbed out of a late model Taurus. That car had the Dixie horn?

She angled her head back into the car and made the toot-the-horn arm motion and the horn blared again. She laughed and slapped her knee at the repeated sound. Yes, that was the car. Everyone in the parking lot turned her way and had mouths hanging open, staring. The trunk popped and she went to the back, grabbed an avocado green hard-sided suitcase, circa 1975, and set it down. Reaching back in, she pulled out a large cardboard box that, from my elevated angle, I could see was filled with liquor bottles. She placed this on the ground next. Lastly, she lifted out a huge watermelon. Oh man, this was going to be a serious road trip.

This was not a woman to underestimate. She had to be strong as an ox to lug a watermelon of that size when she probably weighed ninety pounds soaking wet. I had no doubt she could drink any one of us under the table based on her trip supplies. This woman had been a Roller Doll? She marched right over to JT, who stood on the curb, phone to his ear and mouth on the ground and handed him the watermelon. He fumbled with his coffee, his phone and the large fruit, completely stunned. When Esther turned back to the Dixie car, JT was mumbling to himself. It was probably a good thing I wasn't a lip reader.

Aunt Velma and Goldie piled out of the RV and I followed, albeit a little less enthusiastically.

"Only you, Goldie West, would drive an RV that looks like a giant silver dildo," Esther Millhouse commented, hands on hips and shaking her head.

JT spewed coffee in a three-foot radius, then muttered something I could definitely understand without having to read his lips.

"Put that watermelon inside for me, young man," Esther dictated. Probably knowing he couldn't just hand the thing back to the woman without appearing rude, he just did as he was told. He gave me a look that screamed *what the fuck?*

"Daphne, come meet Esther." I didn't have a choice but to join my aunt and meet the woman since she was going to be spending the next few days with us.

"Hello, Esther." I shook her tiny hand and tried not to cry out when she gave me a death grip squeeze.

"I've heard all about you," she replied. "This is going to be great. I love a good trip with the girls, and that man, hoo wee. Have any of you claimed him yet, because it's been a long time since I've had myself a man like that."

Out of the corner of my eye, I'd seen JT step out of the RV, but at the woman's words, he backpedaled right back inside. Perhaps he was afraid he was going to get his ass pinched. I tried not to grin.

"I've already claimed my man, Esther. You were at the wedding forty years ago," Goldie said.

Esther sniffed. "How about you, Velma?"

"Carl's all the man I need right now, Esther." Based on the way they humped like rabbits, I couldn't imagine her having enough strength for another.

"Hmm, it's just you and me, kid," she eyed me like a boxer across a ring. "So, who is that beefcake?"

"JT, stop hiding and come out here," Aunt Velma called.

Ducking his head, he stepped out of the RV and tried to look like he wasn't dreading the next few minutes. "Ma'am." He nodded at Esther, who was taking in every inch of the man like a sex-crazed woman at an all-male revue.

"JT had a little problem with his motorcycle in Bozeman and we're going to drop him off at Sturgis on the way."

Esther nodded smartly. "Saw the sad thing on the trailer. Heading there for vacation?"

JT ran his hand over the back of his neck, clearly uncomfortable. "Something like that."

"Well, let's not stand here in the McDonald's parking lot all day, we've got sights to see." She clapped, then rubbed her hands together gleefully.

"Only one thing left to get. Grab the crate from the back seat, will you, hot stuff?"

JT's brows went up so high they disappeared beneath his hair. Silently, he went over to the Taurus, opened the rear door and leaned in. All four of us watched his backside as he did so.

Esther eyed me carefully. "Velma said you missed a candle festival in Tibet?"

"Thailand," I replied.

She pursed her lips. "I don't know why you'd have to do that; there's a candle store right in the mall."

At the sound of a snarling wildcat, I turned to JT. He held up a small pet traveling crate by the handle, the plastic container swaying all by itself. Hissing and hideous meowing came from within. He carried it out away from his body and his eyebrows hadn't come down out of his hair.

Once JT closed the back door, the car left, the wheels squealing as they rounded the turn beside the drive-thru.

"What on earth?" Goldie asked. I wasn't sure if she was asking after the wild animal or Mario Andretti.

Esther swatted the air. "Oh, that's just Tigger, my cat. He doesn't take to strangers. Just put him inside. I'll get my bag. Daphne, get the box of liquor. Ooh, this is going to be so much fun!"

With that, she grabbed the Samsonite and climbed into the RV after JT, who held the cat crate like it contained a ticking time bomb.

Left standing in the parking lot, I looked at Goldie and Aunt Velma. I leaned in and whispered, "Why is she coming with us again?"

"She's a close friend of ours and she's a hoot."

A hoot. That was one word for her, all right.

"Why can't she just stay with the person who dropped her off? And what's with *Wild Kingdom*?"

Kids and cats. I didn't much like either.

"It was her grandson and he and his family are heading out on the rodeo circuit in a day or two. He can't take care of a cat."

"He made his grandmother get her own bags out of the trunk?" What kind of child was that? I figured she'd have beaten the crap out of the kid for bad manners.

"You think Esther Millhouse is going to let anyone help her with things like that?" Goldie asked, cleaning out a fingernail.

"She had JT help her," I countered.

"That's only because she wanted to look at his ass," Aunt Velma replied.

Smart woman.

"Let's get a move on. Time's a wastin'," Esther shouted from the RV.

Aunt Velma grinned while Goldie rolled her eyes. "Lord above, we haven't even left the parking lot yet."

Once settled in, Aunt Velma and Goldie were in front, Esther standing between them—she was so small she didn't even need to crouch to see out the windshield. JT and I were in the same spots in the back.

"Does anyone want anything to eat before we go?" Goldie asked.

"Oooh, I'll take one of those new grilled wraps they have. I've heard all about them," Esther told her.

Goldie maneuvered the RV around the building, cars honking at us, which had me glancing out the front. As she moved into the drive-thru lane, I got a little nervous, darted a glance at JT. "Um, Goldie," I called.

"I want one with ranch and all those those yummy bacon bits in there—"

Esther kept yakking and yakking the closer we worked our way toward the drive-thru, Goldie not stopping.

"Goldie, we can't take this through—" I called out.

"Oh shit," JT muttered and launched himself at me, putting his arm up in the male 'stop short' maneuver with his arm across my chest. Needless to say, he got a handful and then some. One of my nipples was very well protected beneath his warm palm.

Whack!

Goldie slammed on the brakes right after the front of the RV directly above the windshield smashed into the steel height restriction bar for the drive-thru.

JT glanced at me, several distinct expressions crossing his face all at once. *Is she crazy? Did that just happen? They're real.* The last was confirmed when he glanced down at my breasts before he lowered his arm.

"Holy hell in a hand basket," Goldie muttered, turning off the motor. Swiveling around in her chair toward us, she hollered, "Are you all right back there?"

I narrowed my eyes at JT and moved away from him, reliving the feel of him groping me. My nipples tingled and places further south perked right up.

"We're fine," I grumbled, not sure if I was mad he'd copped a feel or mad that he'd stopped. The man had tased me and I had the hots for him. Sheesh.

We piled out of the RV to assess the damage. Sure enough, the bar that kept oversized vehicles from going through the drive-thru was leaning against the top of the RV, the metal portion above the windshield was dented in, a perfect shape of a black pipe across the entire front.

"Huh," Aunt Velma said, hands on hips.

"Well, I'll be. Those things *are* meant for something," Esther unnecessarily added.

"Why do they have those stupid things up there, anyway?" Goldie asked at the same time, her dangly earrings swaying as she shook her head.

"So you don't run into the top of the building by the window where you pay and get your food. See," I pointed to the side of the McDonald's. "There's a big overhang."

"Huh," Goldie repeated.

JT just sighed. "Goldie, are you good to drive?" I had a feeling he was a little skeptical, but didn't let it show.

"Sure," she replied.

"Fine, then I'll stand back there"—he thumbed behind us—"and guide you so you can back up. I'd like to get to Sturgis sometime this week."

She nodded and opened the door.

"Just don't run me over," he replied, probably very serious.

"Young man, I've been driving an RV like this for years," Goldie countered.

He just glanced up at the drive-thru bar, then back at her as if that statement held little value to him.

Goldie pursed her lips but didn't say anything.

I figured it was safer for me out of the RV, so I went to stand with JT. Esther took her big handbag and went inside the restaurant, presumably to get her chicken wrap.

JT did his usual cop routine and signaled for a driver to back up with arm motions similar to guiding an airplane away from a gate. Once that was done, there was room for Goldie to get out of the drive-thru lane.

"So, Thailand?" he asked, signaling to Goldie in her side view mirror it was clear to back up.

I crossed my arms, not sure where he was going with this. "Thailand."

He rolled his eyes as he held up his hand for Goldie to stop. "I don't think that's far enough," he replied. "It's like a road trip with the Three Stooges."

I couldn't help but grin because his comparison was dead on. I guess Aunt Velma would be Curly. "Why don't we just drop you at the airport so you can get a rental car and be free of this fiasco?" I asked, knowing he wanted to run away screaming right about now.

"I'd walk through this parking lot asking for a ride right now, even that older couple with the Iowa tags wearing matching Yellowstone sweatshirts, I'm that desperate." He sighed, torn between two terrible options. "It's my bike. I can't leave my bike with the Three Stooges."

I glanced at the mangled motorcycle secured to the trailer.

"Is it that or whatever secret Goldie's got on you?"

His jaw tightened, but he didn't respond. He wasn't thrilled to be on this road trip and it showed, but the mention of what Goldie knew about him had his face going blank, his eyes darken, lips in a grim line. It was like he put a wall up. What *did* Goldie have on him?

We walked back to the side door of the RV and JT opened it, letting me enter first. He had no intention of answering my question, and perhaps I didn't want to know. As I looked back at him over my shoulder, he was staring at my ass. Was it my ass he was ogling or Silky Tangles'?

CHAPTER 6

"Goldie, interstate ninety was that way," I called to the front.

Esther was in the recliner, fully reclined. She was so small her feet didn't even dangle off. The cat carrier was next to her on the floor and all was silent from within. "We're stopping at Pompey's Pillar first."

JT perked up at that. He'd been lying down on the narrow bench seat, eyes closed, one leg on the floor, the other knee bent. One broad shoulder hung off the side. It was a very good view, and very distracting. For being such a pain in the ass, he certainly wasn't a pain on the eyes.

"Why?" I asked. Why in the world did anyone from Montana want to stop at a big rock and see William Clark's signature—of Lewis and Clark fame—carved in it from 1806? We'd all been there, done that at some point in our lives, usually in middle school on a field trip. It wasn't too far out of the way from the highway we needed to take, perhaps thirty miles each way, but at the rate we were going, we'd never get to Sturgis.

Esther leaned down and picked up her big black handbag,

dug around and pulled out a little blue book. "It's my national park passport. I've been to Pompey's Pillar a handful of times but never got the stamp."

"What are you talking about? What stamp?"

"Here," Esther said, tossing me the little book like an expert southpaw pitcher. I fumbled as I caught it and checked it out. JT sat up and ran a hand through his unruly hair.

On the front it read National Park Passport in big gold letters. Inside there were indeed stamps, like a postage cancellation, in the shape of a circle, with the name of the place curved across the top, the location across the bottom and a date in the middle. One page had a stamp from Harpers Ferry, West Virginia, another from Exit Glacier, Alaska, and another from Arches National Park in Utah.

"We're going there to just get a stamp for your little book?" I asked, surprised by the shallowness of the visit. "Don't you want to see the signature on the rock? "

She waved her hand nonchalantly, which somehow made her second chin wobble. "Been there, done that. I've even got the t-shirt. Actually, I do. I just want the stamp."

JT held up a hand. "Hold on. I need to get to Sturgis. I can't go driving to a two-hundred-year-old signature which we don't actually look at it so you can get a stamp for your collection. I don't have time for any of this." He sounded cranky and I didn't blame him. The way his jaw tightened as if he was holding back his true feelings, which most likely involved quite a few swear words strung together, was actually really hot. No. Don't think that way. *He thinks you're a porn star and he tased you.*

"It's only a little out of the way," Esther replied, swiping her hand through the air in a casual *whatever* gesture. She sure liked to talk with her hands. "Look, it's close to five." She glanced at her wrist. "It's time for a drink." She kicked the recliner back into its closed position, shimmied her small frame out of the seat and went to snoop in her cardboard box, bottles clinking as she did.

JT stormed to the front of the RV and crouched down to talk to Goldie. His jeans molded snuggly across his ass. God, I was mentally stalking the man. If he knew the direction of my thoughts—or at least my wandering eyes—he'd probably go postal. Or maybe he'd jump me since he thought I was Silky Tangles.

The only thing we had going for us was that we were driving east. The only bad thing was that we were headed for North Dakota, not South Dakota. Omaha was east of Bozeman so we were technically getting closer, although if we were playing the Hot and Cold game, we'd only be heading toward Warm.

Whatever Goldie said to JT was lost on me, the RV too loud to hear, and Esther was clinking bottles around like she worked in a saloon, but he turned around and came back, eyes narrowed. He wasn't happy. He stood to stand next to Esther, who continued to work her mixology. "Okay, if we stop and get your stamp, that'll take, what, five minutes?" He towered over the older woman, but she wasn't cowered in the slightest.

"Plus a bathroom break," Esther said, pouring a drink into a plastic cup she found in one of the small cabinets above the tiny stove. "Here." She held out the cup to JT. "You look like you could use one first."

He eyed it for a moment, sighed, then murmured, "What the hell." A big swig later, he slumped back down into his spot across from me. Wincing, he looked at Esther. "What is this, jet fuel?"

"It'll put hair on your chest, all right." Esther chuckled before gulping down half her drink, eyeing the man like she had x-ray vision. "Five minutes for the stamp. Five minutes for a potty break. Then we're done."

* * *

POMPEY'S PILLAR was pretty interesting, if you're into history. A signature that explorers carved in a rock along the banks of a river they'd used as their mode of transportation—no doubt they'd have taken the interstate like us if it had existed in 1806—was the sole reason it was a National Landmark. This part of Montana was far from the mountains, therefore it was a little more arid, scrubby and dry. The Yellowstone River meandered through the vast expanse of...nothing. So when we pulled into the visitor center, we weren't surprised it wasn't overly crowded. The sun was getting lower in the west, the day cooler now.

Esther was the first out of the RV, passport book in hand, motivation in her step. JT, a good hundred pounds heavier than Esther, was a little slower moving, clearly whatever she'd mixed in his cocktail had mellowed him out. We only made it halfway to the entrance before she was on her way back. "Bad news," she grumbled. She looked clearly disappointed and had the strong aroma of a distillery about her. "Visitor Center's closed for the night."

"Great!" JT clapped his hands together. It was his turn to be gleeful. "We can make it to Sturgis by one, two in the morning. I just need some dinner and I'll be sober enough to drive."

"What?" Esther asked. "Dinner, sure. I'm hungry. But we're not leaving! I don't have my stamp."

"You can come another time. You only live a few hours away."

JT and Esther would be nose to nose if she were only a foot taller. He could knock her down with his pinky finger, but Esther was holding her own. She was like a honey badger fighting a big lion. I knew who was going to win this battle and anyone who'd seen a documentary on honey badgers knew as well.

"No way." Esther shook her head, curls springing and bouncing. "We're here. It's time to eat, then we'll spend the night and get the stamp first thing in the morning."

"I'm not sure what kind of food's around here. We're kind of in the middle of nowhere," I said, enjoying the clear blue sky that went on forever. There wasn't a fast food restaurant in sight.

"Then we head back to Billings," JT countered.

"That's going the wrong way!" Goldie added.

"I need that stamp," Esther countered, her voice louder.

"You're like a damn honey badger with that stamp, Esther," Velma said, tossing her hands up in the air. Wow, Aunt Velma and I had thought the same thing about how persistent the woman could be. We must have seen that same documentary. "I mean, really? It's a dang stamp. Let it go."

JT smiled at Aunt Velma with blatant relief. "Thank you."

"I'm in agreement, but we need to find some food," Goldie added. "I'm starved."

"If you hadn't literally hit that drive-thru we'd have eaten those wraps and wouldn't need to stop," Esther glared at Goldie.

Goldie arched a brow, but kept quiet.

"Why can't we just eat what we brought in the RV and be on our way? You guys can stop here on your way back when neither JT nor I are with you," I offered, trying to be diplomatic. I didn't want to stay overnight to get the silly stamp either, and I was hungry.

Everyone was quiet for a moment.

"I guess that's all right," Esther said, although fairly glumly.

"I guess we don't have to head back to Billings if we can take a backroad to cut down to Sturgis," JT said, compromising.

"Fine, then. I'll whip something together," Aunt Velma said, already walking back to the RV, her words carrying over her shoulder.

"Oh, no. You burn water. I'll cook," Goldie ran to catch up and keep pace with Velma. She was right. If Aunt Velma got near the food, we'd either starve from eating rabbit food or wouldn't eat at all because she'd ruined it.

Esther moseyed along behind them, obviously disappointed she didn't get her stamp.

Once inside, Aunt Velma took over driving while Goldie began digging through the grocery bags of food to pull a meal together. "What the hell?" she muttered, shaking her head. She was leaning over, head in the tiny, college dorm room sized fridge.

She pulled out a—

"What the hell?" Esther repeated.

—ceramic garden gnome.

"That Zach. I tell you." Goldie shook her head and rolled her eyes. "He's obsessed with this ridiculous gnome. Wow, it's really cold."

She placed it on the small table in front of me. It was about a foot tall, big white beard, red jacket, creepy smile. I swear it was leering at me.

"Why did he put that thing in the fridge?" Esther asked.

Goldie returned to her work, pulling out cold cuts and condiments and started to build sandwiches. "He got it at a garage sale last summer. You wouldn't believe the stories that gnome has. It leads quite a life. Last month it went to Alaska."

I looked at the devilish guy. "Zach wants it to go on the road trip with us?"

Goldie shrugged. "All I know is that we need to keep it

safe until we get home. Even though he left it with us, that little guy's special to Zach. Even named it."

"Well?" Esther prodded when Goldie didn't say more. "Don't keep us guessing." She went over to the pet carrier, squatted down and opened it. I was waiting for a cat to leap out and attack her, but when Esther reached in, she pulled out a bright orange tabby cat. Climbing into the recliner, she put it on her lap. After spinning a few times and kneading her legs, it curled up and went to sleep.

"George," Goldie replied, eyeing the cat.

JT just shook his head and stared at George the Gnome. "How hard can it be to babysit a garden gnome?"

The RV lurched from hitting a pothole and George teetered on the table. I grabbed it before it could plummet onto the linoleum floor. I exhaled, relieved it hadn't broken. "Yeah, how hard can it be?"

Over the next hour, turkey sandwiches were made by Goldie while Velma drove on a state road back toward interstate ninety, meeting up with it southeast of Billings to get us back on track toward Sturgis, and ultimately Omaha. Esther was the drinks lady, mixing fruity cocktails for all of us—except Velma—to go with our meal. Without a place to sleep, the cat had gone off into the back bedroom and hadn't been seen since.

"If you aren't going to eat your fruit, you might as well drink it. It's important to have a healthy diet." Esther returned to her recliner, her drink in the little built in cup holder, paper plate in her lap. Goldie sat with me at the little dinette and JT across from us.

"How long is your vacation?" Goldie asked JT.

"Ten days." He chomped on a chip.

"That's a nice bike you have," Goldie added, clearly trying for small talk.

JT just glared at me, remembering I was the one who had

broken it. I glared at Goldie, not thankful she'd reminded JT *why* he was riding with us. I took a big gulp of my drink. My eyes watered. Wow, it was strong and had plenty of vitamin C.

"I like it," JT finally said. "I guess I have to thank you for arranging with Bob to have it fixed."

Goldie just shrugged. She'd put on a hot pink hoodie over her t-shirt. "It's the least we could do. Right, Daphne?"

"Right," I agreed quickly. "What kinds of things do you do at the Rally?"

"More like *who*," murmured Goldie.

"What?" I asked, confused. We hit another pothole and I bounced up in my seat.

Goldie shook her head as she sipped her own drink. "What's in this, pineapple?" she called to Esther.

"Secret ingredient. Not telling," Esther replied. I really didn't care what she put in it. It was tasty and if it could numb my senses, it would be all the better.

"I've never been before, but friends of mine are already there and invited me to catch up." JT took a healthy gulp of his drink. "My days off were short notice."

"Oh?" Goldie asked. "You mean your trip wasn't planned?"

I swear JT blushed, but couldn't tell for sure. It was starting to get dark and the RV's lights weren't overly bright. Things were starting to get a little blurry around the edges from the drink.

"I got the time off because of that call out on Baxter Road," JT murmured.

"You were on that call?" Velma asked from the driver's seat. She might have had her eyes on the road, but her ears were on the conversation.

JT nodded, his mouth a thin line. "It was pretty bad. All of us who responded were given some leave."

I looked at Goldie. She wasn't smiling. "What call?" I asked.

"Some drunk driver on the wrong side of the road. You should tell it, JT, not me." Goldie took a bite of her sandwich, letting JT take his time to respond.

"A family was killed. It wasn't pretty. End of story."

My sandwich felt like lead in my stomach. "Oh. I'm sorry."

"Now you're going to go to Sturgis for a little fun," Goldie said, her voice filled once again with verve. She even waggled her eyebrows.

I darted a glance at JT.

He grinned. "We'll see." He turned those dark eyes on me, looked at me in a way that had my toes curling in my sneakers. "We'll see," he repeated. "What about you, Daphne?"

I pointed a chip at myself. "Me?"

"Yeah, you. What's this with Thailand?"

I arched a brow. "Now you believe me?"

He shrugged, tipped up the corner of his lip. "You have to admit, it's a good front for being Silky Tangles."

"Silky Tangles?" Esther asked. She narrowed her eyes at me. "I thought you looked familiar. You're pretty smart going off and doing that job on the sly. I could pull it off if I was a few years younger. My breasts aren't quite what they used to be."

Goldie chuckled into her drink. JT shifted uncomfortably, possibly from the visual Esther shared or indigestion. How Esther knew who Silky Tangles was had me putting down the remainder of my sandwich for good.

The RV came to a stop. "Okay, people. I need a break. I'm starving," Velma said as she turned off the engine and came into the back to join us. I glanced out the front window. We were in a Wal-Mart parking lot, the farthest spots from the entrance.

"Where are we?" Goldie asked, glancing out the side window.

"Hardin," Velma replied, making herself a sandwich.

"I'll drive," Esther piped in.

"Oh no, you don't," JT said. "You've had way too much to drink and that secret ingredient you mentioned has to be some kind of moonshine. Unfortunately, none of us can drive except Velma."

"In that case, I say we spend the night here, get schnock-ered, then head out in the morning," Esther said. She worked her way out of the recliner and grabbed everyone's cup, added one from the cabinet for Velma, and lined them up on the tiny countertop.

JT glanced at his watch, rolled his eyes. "We've been gone ten hours and only made it two hundred miles. At this rate, we'll be in Sturgis in three days."

"Then have yourself another drink. It'll change your whole outlook." She handed him a full cup.

"We're in Montana, one of the prettiest places on earth and our view is the Wal-Mart parking lot," Goldie grumbled.

"Just for tonight, GG," Velma commented, accepting the cup Esther offered her and taking a big sip. "Wow, that's a serious drink. I'm too tired to search for a campground. Besides, you can always park your camper overnight at a Wal-Mart."

I wasn't getting involved in this one; I was along for the ride. I knew going in that this wasn't going to be a straight shot to Omaha since nothing with Aunt Velma ever went as planned. I'd hoped, but deep down, knew that I was doomed. It was going to be an adventure; I just didn't know what it would entail. JT, on the other hand, had to come to the real-ization that Sturgis might not actually happen. Maybe he had come to terms with this because when Esther handed him his drink refill, he tossed it back like a fraternity brother.

73

"Let's play a game," Esther said, settling back into the recliner.

I had no interest in playing Quarters and Truth or Dare with this group would give me nightmares.

"What game?" Goldie asked.

"What's the one word you hate?"

"That's a game?" Aunt Velma asked.

"Sure," Esther countered. "I'll start. I hate the word tabernacle."

"Tabernacle?" Goldie repeated, shaking her head. "What on earth is wrong with that?"

"It's the 'nacle' part. It just sounds weird. I mean, it's just a funny sounding word for a church. What's the point?"

Okay, the word *was* weird.

"You go next, Daphne," Esther said.

I thought for a moment. "Slacks." Everyone glanced at me. "What? Old grandpas wear slacks, so I hate it when I read in books these thirty-year-old hot guys are wearing slacks. It ruins it." I took a gulp of my drink. "Pants is better."

The ladies considered it and somewhat grudgingly agreed.

"I don't like the word demure," Aunt Velma said.

Goldie frowned. "Why not? What on earth is wrong with it?"

"I don't know if it's supposed to be said like 'I want *more*,' or like a 'mural'."

"I say demure," Goldie said, using the *mural* sound.

"Well I say the opposite. Demure," Velma countered with the *more* version.

"It's like caramel. Is it car-mel or car-a-mel?" Goldie asked.

We all piped up with our different versions.

"Your turn, hot stuff," Esther said. We all looked to JT.

"Panties," he replied, taking a sip of his drink.

My mouth fell open. So did the others.

"Why?" I wondered.

He shrugged. "Just don't like saying it."

"If not panties, what should they be then?"

He was facing all of us, but his gaze was on me. "On the floor."

$\mathcal{T}$wo hours later, JT and I sat across from each other —still—and questioned our sanity. I was forming a little ass groove in the cushion beneath me. Goldie and Velma had gone to sleep, the two of them sharing the small bedroom in the back, only after Esther grabbed the cat, who hadn't been happy about losing its bed. How Goldie and Velma fit in that bed was beyond me, but that was their problem. What *was* my problem was that I could hear them snoring through the closed door. Esther had made it one drink longer than the other two and had conked out in the recliner, her head tilted back, mouth open, cat asleep in lap. She, too, snored and sounded like a buzz saw.

"I've never heard anything like it," JT said, wincing when Esther's snore turned into a snort.

I put my hands up to my ears. "I'm not drunk enough to survive this."

JT stood, held out his hand. "Let's get out of here."

I stared at him for a moment, long enough to suffer through a chorus of commingled snores. I reached out, took his hand and we fled the RV.

Once we'd walked far enough away to have the buzz saw silenced, we paused. His hand was big, engulfing mine, but his touch was gentle. Warm. Very reassuring for someone who'd tased me. Oh yeah, the guy was a jerk. It was just hard to remember that when his hand felt good. And that was just his hand. So I tugged it from his grip and stepped back.

The night was cool, but I didn't need a jacket. The parking lot was deserted, the bright halide lights set JT in harsh shadows. He ran a hand over his face. "How do you handle that?" He tilted his head toward the RV.

"Thailand."

"And when you were younger?"

A slight breeze swept my hair into my face and I tucked it behind my ear. "Boarding school, college, career."

"The only way I'm going back in there is if I get more to drink first." He thumbed over his shoulder toward the RV.

"All right, then where?"

JT glanced around. "Bowling alley?"

I turned to where he looked, saw the flickering neon sign in the squat building next to the Walmart. Chippers Lanes' lot was full. It appeared *the* place to be in Hardin. I shrugged. "You want to bowl, Detective?"

He grinned, ran his hand over the back of his neck. "Bowling's best when you're not sober, so why the hell not? I promise not to pinch your ass like Frank."

Pinch? No. Pat or hmm...spank? Yes, please.

"It's not my sport, but I'm up for it." Anything was better than the snoring Three Stooges.

We were lucky to get a spare lane, the place hopping with league games. The sound of pins being knocked down and heavy metal rock music filled the air along with a large cloud of cigarette smoke. The place was total vintage. The only thing that had been updated since 1965 was the game computers that did the scoring math for you. Young and old wore ridiculously bad shirts with team names like Holy Rollers and Dolls with Balls across the front. I sat and put on my rental shoes as JT got us some beers from the bar.

"I hope you like light beer," he said as he placed two plastic cups filled with beer and foam on the table above our lane. "We might need a few more to make it through the night."

Thinking of the snoring, I had to agree. I was definitely buzzed by Esther's liberal helpings of mystery drinks and grinned as I remembered the stupid rhyme from college: *Beer before liquor, never felt sicker. Liquor before beer, you're in the clear.* At least I wouldn't be hungover. "Great idea."

After JT traded his shoes for the rentals, I ogled his broad shoulders and back muscles flexing beneath his t-shirt as he bent down to put them on.

"Want to tell me what Goldie's got on you?"

He glanced up from his crouch as he tied a shoelace, eyes devoid of emotion. "What do you mean?"

I went over and picked out a ball from the rack, tested the weight, the space of the finger holes. "Come on, she's got something about you at Sturgis. You wouldn't be here otherwise."

He gave his shoulders a little shrug. "So?"

"So I want to know what it is."

"Nosy, are we?" His mouth quirked up at the corner. Somehow, he didn't seem as tense as a moment ago.

I found the ball I wanted to use; a bright blue covered in silver sparkles. I placed it in the ball return. "What happens in Hardin, stays in Hardin."

He stood to his full height, went to find his own ball. "All right. You heard about Bob, the guy who's going to fix my bike."

I looked down at the linoleum tiles at my feet. "Yeah, about that—"

"I've had too much to drink to be pissed at the moment about the bike."

"Oh."

"Bob, the mechanic, fixed me up and I was going to miss out."

The liquor I'd drank felt sour in my stomach. I took a step back, realizing I was out of my element. Of course, he had a girl lined up. He wasn't hard on the eyes—even the older ladies in the lane beside ours couldn't keep from ogling him. If he broke bowling etiquette and veered into their lane, I might never see him again.

"That's *all* Goldie has on you? A blind date?"

He didn't say anything, just placed a red ball next to mine. The group in the lane next to ours broke out in shouts of "Turkey, turkey!" I had no idea what it meant, but they obviously did and it appeared to be a good thing.

"All I'm going to share," he responded. There was a story there, the journalist in me could see it, but it didn't seem like I was going to get it out of him, even with liquor.

"You should feel lucky then, a blind date's nothing. My friend Violet wrote a romance book and Goldie knew about it and published it behind her back."

He frowned. "So? Sounds like she was helping."

"Goldie gave her the pen name Cherry Bottoms."

His mouth fell open. "Oh shit."

"When her daughter-in-law started dating again—her husband died—Goldie sent the man a box of sex toys and condoms."

The corner of his mouth ticked up. "What's she got on you?"

"Nothing. I'm not in town enough."

"That's right, Silky. Your job keeps you away."

"At least I don't have to be fixed up on a blind date," I countered, bitterness lacing every word. I couldn't even keep

Roger, the philandering computer guy. He never once said I looked like Silky Tangles.

"The blind date's name is Sarah. She's a dentist from Denver looking to settle down, not some guy named Benny from the Trekker Truck Stop with a DVD player."

My mouth fell open at his insult as I spun on my rental shoes and went over to the computer game display and sat down. I couldn't compare to a dentist from Denver. I had no real home, I traveled fifty weeks out of the year and lived out of a suitcase. I pasted on a fake smile. "Ah, you're looking for the whole picket fence, are you?"

"Girls like you are larger than life on screen, gorgeous in person, but only good for a quick tumble."

"What do you have against porn stars anyway? It sounds like you know all about Silky Tangles and have seen all her movies since you know about the whole *Stuffed and Cuffed* thing. You can't hate porn that much."

"It suits its purpose, but I'm not interested in a woman like you."

I shifted in my seat. He either believed I really was Silky Tangles or he was completely delusional. "Right, a woman just like me fucked up your life from a DVD?" I shook my head. "Whatever." I typed his name into the computer keyboard to keep from punching him once again. My only advantage was that he probably didn't have his stun gun on him.

"McHottie?" He moved to lean over my shoulder. His arm came around to type one handed. His body heat radiated, his clean scent circled around and I felt his breath next to my ear. He was very...close. Was it hot in here? "Okay, Silky, let's play."

I tilted my head up to the electronic scoresheet. Sure enough, my bowling name was Silky.

Since his name was entered first, he bowled first,

knocking down eight, then waited for the lane to reset the two remaining pins.

He clearly had a delineation in his mind between good girls and bad girls. One was fine for the night, the other for a lifetime.

"Do you really think this Sarah woman is interested in finding a husband at the Sturgis Motorcycle Rally? Seriously?" I leaned back in the plastic swivel chair, my legs tucked under the table, my arms folded over my chest. "She's looking for the guy version of Silky Tangles."

The ball popped out of the return. He picked it up, chucked the ball down the lane, knocking over the remaining pins.

"Spare," he said. "What about you? You looking for Mr. Right?"

The lane reset and it was my turn. I stood. "Don't you mean Mr. Right Now?"

I picked up my blue ball and lined up to go.

"You have what, three or four Mr. Right Now's while filming. It's not like Mr. Right's going to want to come home to you."

Wow. That was...cruel and I wasn't even a porn star. "That's such a double standard." I faced the lane, lined up and swung. The ball slid down the lane smoothly then took out all the pins.

"Strike," I replied. "I'm going to get a pitcher." I didn't look back, just headed for the bar. It was snoring in the RV or jackass JT. I chose neither.

* * *

"You've got some pretty hot moves," a man to my right said. I turned. Twenties, Wrangler jeans, snug t-shirt, cowboy hat. Not half bad.

Not interested.

"Um, thanks." I turned back to watch the bartender fill the pitcher. "Bowling's fun."

"I don't mean bowling." He moved in a smidgen closer, which put him definitely in my space. He had quite the roving eye which seemed to stop squarely on my breasts.

Another guy approached, leered. He wasn't half bad looking either, but he gave me the creeps. "I'm Jared. My idiot friend here is Paul."

I nodded vaguely, eyed the bartender who was at the tap. "Hi."

"What brings you to Montana?" Jared asked.

"I live here." No way was I giving more information than that.

"In Hardin? Not a chance." He shook his head and chuckled. "We would've known." Anyone moving to a town the size of Hardin would be big news. Hardin made Bozeman look like New York City.

"Nope. Not Hardin."

"Here with that guy?" Paul asked, tilting his chin toward the lanes.

"Yup." I leaned forward on the glossy wood bar and focused on the bartender, willing him to work his way back to me.

"That's okay. We don't mind sharing." He moved in closer. "We know you like it." His words had me whipping my head around to look at him. The guy actually waggled his eyebrows. Jared just grinned.

Oh great. They thought I was Silky Tangles.

"Look, guys, I'm not who you think I am."

Jared's gaze raked down my body, grinned. "Right. Incognito." He looked left and right, leaned close and lowered his voice. "We won't tell anyone. We promise, don't we, Paul?"

Jared's leer matched Paul's sleazy look. They were

certainly not thinking pure thoughts at the moment. "Yeah, we promise."

"Look, guys, I'm flattered and all, but I'm not into sharing."

An arm came around my shoulder from behind. "Neither am I."

I tensed before realizing it was JT and relaxed into his hold, his hand warm on my upper arm. Even through the smoke and the spilled beer aroma, I picked up JT's clean scent. I could handle brushing off a guy because I never really considered myself much of a catch, but two guys who thought I was a sexual acrobat and into ménage on film, was something else entirely. Silky Tangles seemed to have a lot of followers and they were all in Montana. Actually, because of me, the real Silky Tangles was probably stalker free. Wherever she was.

"Right, baby?" He leaned in and whispered close to my ear. I felt his breath fan my nape. The possessiveness I heard in JT's voice was not only a relief, but a total turn-on. He was a complete asshat, but it felt good to have a guy watch out for me. Even if it was a complete act.

"You're going to play hard to get? Seriously? Is this how you treat your fans?" Paul asked.

"Is this how you treat women?" I countered, hand on hip.

"You're not a woman, you're a porn star. At least show us your tits." Jared reached out to tuck a finger under the hem of my t-shirt.

That's when I grabbed his wrist and twisted it sideways with my left hand while I punched him in the nose with my right.

After that, all hell broke loose.

Paul said something nasty, JT tackled him to the ground, breaking a table in the process. Jared covered his bleeding nose and called me a really offensive name not even used in porn flicks. By the time I kneed him in the groin, the bartender had come around the bar to grab my arm.

Of course, it would have just been a bar brawl and we wouldn't have been arrested if the Hardin police department wasn't in lane four and cranky from losing to the volunteer fire department the next lane over. Team Bowl Movement took us to jail while team Ebowla dealt with Jared's broken nose.

CHAPTER 8

"*A*rrested twice in three days, Daphne, is not something to be proud of." Aunt Velma's voice was what woke me. My head felt like a bowling ball, my tongue needed to be shaved and I smelled like beer. I'd open my eyes wider than narrow slits, but I was afraid the overhead light might blind me.

"Don't talk so loud," I groaned.

"Here."

I opened one eye carefully and saw four pills resting in Aunt Velma's palm along with a tiny paper cup of water. I took the pills and guzzled the water, although it was only about a swallow's worth.

"We go to sleep and the next thing I know I'm being called down to the police station. Again."

Police station? Oh shit.

I sat up and looked around and wished I hadn't. So much for stupid college rhymes. My head was about to explode. I was once again in a jail cell, these cinder block walls painted a lovely shade of mauve. The bed was once again hard and the smell was the same institutional scent as in Bozeman. "Where's JT?"

"Goldie's bailing him out now. I expected you to punch him again, not someone else."

I ran my hand over my hair and felt it sticking out in the back. I felt like road kill and I probably looked like it, too. "JT isn't the only asshat around," I replied dryly.

"You started a bar brawl, Daphne." The sound of her voice had me turning my head. She wasn't angry; she was trying not to laugh.

I cracked a smile, quickly discovering that doing any kind of grinning would make my head hurt too much. "Yeah. Yeah, I did."

"You've got some serious anger management issues."

I closed my eyes and sighed. I was sitting in a jail cell. Again. I definitely had issues.

* * *

WHEN A WOMAN TOOK the Walk of Shame, usually it was after a one-night stand. Since that would be too cool for me—either a guy didn't want me, like Roger, or guys wanted me too much, like those losers at the bowling alley—I'd had to come up with my own kind of personal hell.

Walking out of a police station, hungover, in clothes that reeked of stale booze, my hair snarled in ways not able to be made by man and having to face not only Goldie and Esther Millhouse, but the guy who'd been trying to defend me, well, I'd stooped to a whole new low. I couldn't escape any of them since we were all stuck in the RV together.

"At least you didn't pee yourself this time," Goldie said to me.

I rolled my eyes up into my head. "I didn't pee myself last time," I replied wearily.

"Last time?" Esther asked. This morning she wore a hot pink track suit, her hair in the same perfect ringlets. I worried about her getting too close to an open flame with all the hairspray.

"You wouldn't believe it. She was headed to the airport and—"

Goldie and Esther walked out of the lobby and into the bright sunshine, a few words drifting back as the door closed behind them. *No. JT did that? She did what to him? He did? Of course, she peed her pants.*

"You." JT pointed at me, although he looked too tired to put much anger behind the words. For spending the night in a jail cell, JT didn't look all that bad. Of course, his hair looked good all messed up. Of course, he looked good with whiskers that were twelve hours past a five o'clock shadow. "You are a total menace. I should—"

"What? Taser me?" I was hungover, I had several members of the Hardin police department staring at us from behind the counter and Aunt Velma looming over us, but that didn't mean I was going to stand here and take it. "If you'd just let me get on that damn plane, *none* of this would have happened."

I sliced through the air with my hand.

"You're saying spending the night in jail was my fault?" he asked, his voice incredulous. "You're the one who punched the guy in the face. You have anger management issues."

Aunt Velma just gave me a look that said it all: *See?*

"You tackled the other jerk to the ground like a football linebacker!"

"Boys and girls," Aunt Velma called out, but we ignored her.

"He called you a...." Yeah, the word was bad. At least JT had enough taste not to say it.

"You're only interested in a girl like me for a one-night

87

stand, yet you deck a guy for wanting the exact same thing. You can't have it both ways, JT."

He ran his hand over his neck and looked at me with bloodshot eyes.

"You want a one-night stand with Daphne?"

JT at least had the grace to blush at the question.

"Aunt Velma," I whined. "Can you just give us a minute?"

"Why? If I leave, the nice police officers over there are still going to get to hear you both."

JT and I turned to look at the men watching us like we were prizefighters, most likely wondering which of us was going to throw the first punch.

I lifted my hands in surrender. "Forget it. Let's just get out of here."

One of the police officers cleared his throat. "Can we get your autograph before you go, Miss Tangles?"

* * *

I OPENED the door to the RV and stepped back as Tigger hissed at me from inside. "Jesus," I muttered. The cat's fur stood on end, the tail straight up and its little kitty fangs hung down like a vampire's. Velma leaned in and looked over my shoulder.

"That cat is feral," she muttered. "Esther, get your crazy cat!"

Esther, a blur of hot pink, came by and scooped up the animal. "She's good attack cat."

Why anyone would want to steal the pickle was beyond me. With the coast clear, I climbed into the RV followed by Aunt Velma, JT taking up the rear.

Esther was back in the recliner, cat in lap. It didn't look overly feral at the moment. Maybe it was schizophrenic instead. Velma settled into the jump seat and JT and I took up our usual spots, me behind the table, him across on the bench seat.

Goldie turned from the little kitchenette and handed JT and me each a cup of coffee.

Wrapping my hands around the hot mug, I sniffed the black brew and felt my headache recede.

"We have a problem," Goldie said.

And the headache was back.

"Oh, which problem?" I asked, taking a tentative sip.

Goldie poured another cup and handed it to Esther. "Can you pour a little whiskey in mine?"

A cellphone dinged. Velma grabbed hers from her purse on the floor between the two front seats. "Oh, it's Carl," she replied. I swear I saw little hearts floating around her head.

Which problem could it possibly be? I was stuck with a chauvinistic asshat, or perhaps it was the feral cat. Maybe it was the pint-sized lush, or was it the nymphomaniac Amazon? Goldie was actually looking pretty tame right about now and that was saying something.

"Put that away, Velma. Carl can live without you for a few minutes longer."

Aunt Velma pursed her lips but put her phone away.

"What's the problem, Goldie?"

"Seniorita is having her girl parts pulled out and we need to go and be with her in the hospital."

JT was slumped low on the bench, his legs stretched out into the aisle, if you could call it that. He just sat there and drank his coffee, not even looking up at what Goldie just said.

"Seniorita? Isn't it *Señorita*?" I wondered aloud.

"Actually, it's Tanya Kolanowski, but that's her roller derby name," Aunt Velma supplied. "She's the oldest woman on the Roller Dolls team, so it's a play on being a senior citizen."

I envisioned Esther with a helmet and knee pads out there on the oval course. "How old is this woman?"

"Forty-two and she's having a hysterectomy. Something weird's going on in there and the plumbing's got to go."

"I'm sorry to hear that, but why is that a problem?" My brain was still a little foggy, but the coffee was helping. A second cup would help even more. I got up to serve myself.

"We need to go to Fargo."

Now JT came alive. "Over my dead body."

"I have to agree with him on this one," I muttered.

The Dixie horn blared, making me wince.

"There's our ride!" Esther stood, dumping the cat onto the floor, where it padded unhappily into the bedroom at the back.

"Ride?" I asked, JT tipping down the metal blinds.

"Esther's grandson is loaning us his car so we can drive to Fargo."

"I thought he was going on the rodeo circuit?"

"Who's *we*?" JT asked warily.

"Goldie, Esther and I," Velma said, picking up her purse.

I held up a hand. "Wait a second. Sit down!" I shouted, the ladies were fluttering around and driving me crazy. They all turned to look at me, probably more surprised I yelled with a hangover than at my cranky tone. "What am I to do with the RV? I'm not driving it to Omaha." *No way in hell.*

"You'll take JT to Sturgis, then drive from there to Fargo to pick us up."

"You want me to drive to Fargo, North Dakota. Are you serious?" The way they stared at me I knew they were.

"I actually like this plan. We can be in Sturgis by the afternoon." JT's color had improved and he was actually smiling.

"Just drop JT off and get to Fargo because you're on the roster as Seniorita's replacement."

"For what, her uterus?" My lady parts were pretty rusty from lack of use, so I doubted she'd want them.

Goldie frowned and Aunt Velma smirked. "For the Women's Flat Track Roller Derby Association's championship game between the Fargo Roller Dolls and the Houston Hell On Wheels."

JT spewed coffee all over himself. He seemed to have a problem with that.

"Are you kidding me?"

"We don't kid about roller derby, Daphne," Esther chided.

"You want me to be in a roller derby competition?"

"You want *Daphne* to do roller derby?" JT asked, amusement lacing every word.

I'd been part of the Minnesota women's hockey team that won the national championship, not once, but twice. No way in hell was I telling that to JT. If he wanted to learn something about me besides my cup size, then he could just ask.

All four of us glared at the man. "What?" he asked, hands up in surrender.

"Your anger issues will come in handy," Esther added, turning back to me with a gleam of maliciousness in her eye.

"If you do this, Daph, then we'll put you on a plane from Fargo back to Bozeman," Velma added. "We'll take the RV down to Omaha from there."

"That's blackmail," I replied, not thrilled they were holding my escape from this ridiculous road trip over me.

"You're the best replacement I can think of." Aunt Velma moved to put her hands on my shoulders. "I wouldn't let just anyone play for the Roller Dolls. You'll do right by the team and make us all proud."

It was one of the sappiest moments I'd ever had with Aunt Velma. She wasn't one to offer platitudes or feelings of any kind, for that matter.

"I've never even played before."

JT said something under his breath that seemed to have something to do with *suicide*, but I couldn't be sure.

"Doesn't matter. You know the rules; I beat them into you when we used to watch it on TV. There will be some practice time in advance. Besides, spending time alone with JT will only build up your angst, and you'll be hell on wheels by the time competition rolls around."

"Every pun intended," Esther added.

This time, JT looked put out.

The Dixie horn blared again. Esther picked up her Samsonite case. "I didn't even get to use the watermelon," she muttered as she left, leaving the door open behind her.

"It's what, about three hundred miles to Sturgis then I can get rid of you." I glared at JT. "Then I have peace and quiet all the way to Fargo."

"Just be there tomorrow night," Esther warned.

"Tomorrow night? Fargo's not around the corner." They just looked at me, not interested in anything but agreement. I sighed loudly. "Fine, fine. I'll do it."

Aunt Velma only nodded her head, but I could tell she was relieved. Both she and Goldie picked up their bags—clearly knowing I'd say yes as they had pre-packed—and dropped kisses on my cheek before fleeing the RV as if it were on fire.

"Text me when you hit the North Dakota line," Aunt Velma called out. Two car doors slammed, then the horn blared one last time for effect and the car peeled out of the police lot.

"God, it's quiet," JT said, the humming of the refrigerator loud now that the ladies were gone.

"I need at least another two cups of coffee," I said. "There's got to be a McDonald's in this town."

JT leaned down and pulled the door shut, then bent his body in half to squeeze behind the wheel. He fiddled with the seat and pushed it back about a foot. "I'll take the first shift driving."

"Fine," I countered. Three hundred miles. That's all I had left with this man. Just breathe!

I climbed into the passenger seat and put on my seatbelt.

Fortunately, in the ladies' haste they left the keys in the ignition. Pulling up to the street, JT waited for traffic, then turned right.

"Um, JT, I think you need to take it—"

The roving pickle scraped alongside a yellow pylon that protected a fire hydrant situated poorly just off the street. The pylon slid down the length of the RV, scraping against the side. Once the RV cleared it, the ear-splitting screech of metal on metal stopped. So did we. JT slammed on the brakes and I jerked against the seatbelt.

"Shit," JT muttered, undid his seatbelt and jumped out of the RV.

I went out my door. Since the damage was on my side, I saw it first. It was like the Titanic hitting the iceberg, metal torn away in parts. Other spots were only dented in and the entire right side of the RV had a new yellow stripe down it. It was a good thing Goldie wasn't here to see this.

"It's a good thing I'll be long gone when Goldie sees this," JT said, his voice grim, repeating my thoughts.

"You are such an asshat!" I shook my head and got back in the passenger seat, buckling my seatbelt with more force than necessary. The condition of the RV was completely irrelevant at this point. Goldie had dented the front quite nicely, I'd added the shape of a motorcycle to the back bumper, and now we were driving the Titanic on wheels. Something else was going to go wrong. It had to. I was just three hundred miles from getting rid of the man, and I needed to remain sane until then.

While I waited for JT to climb back in, I checked my

email on my phone. I clicked on my editor's name in the inbox. He had a job for me in Brazil studying the impacts of cows on the rainforest. I had to be there in a week. I felt relieved knowing I had something lined up, but the idea of heading off to the wilds of Brazil didn't have me all excited. In fact, it made me even more tired.

JT climbed back in and I put my phone away. He put the RV in gear and began driving.

"Coffee," I muttered, ignoring everything else. "If you forget the coffee I will kill you and leave you in the back bedroom to rot."

CHAPTER 9

*C*rossing into Wyoming, I took over at a rest stop. The caffeine had kicked in and I felt functional once again, the hangover cured by Aunt Velma's pills. Perhaps not rested, but I could drive. We hadn't spoken other than to agree to change drivers. JT checked his phone and did some texting.

"Making plans?" I asked.

"Just telling Bob when I should be in."

"What about Sarah?"

"What about her?"

"Got a picture?"

"It wouldn't be a blind date if I had a photo."

I just turned my head and stared at him.

"Fine. No. Bob didn't send one. Why do Velma and Esther think you can do the roller derby thing?"

I glanced at JT, then back at the road. "Changing the topic?"

"Yes." He didn't even try to argue about it.

"Fine. Because I used to play hockey."

"Field hockey with those little skirts? I can see that."

"No, ice hockey. Jeez, can you stop being such a chauvinistic asshole for five minutes?"

"Wow, you said a bad word," he countered, then grinned. "Ice hockey. Tell me all about it. You have my attention for a few more hours."

I sighed. "I played at boarding school in Vermont, then got a scholarship to Minnesota to play there."

"That's it?"

I wasn't telling him about how good the team was. He wouldn't care. "Eight years of hockey compressed into one sentence, so yeah, that's it. Plus, the anger issues I seem to have. Combined, I'll probably do fine."

"Why are they so into it?"

"Aunt Velma and Esther?" He nodded. "They were Roller Dolls back in the seventies. Won a few championships. When I moved in with Aunt Velma, she taught me all about it."

"You grew up with your aunt?"

"*Now* you're curious?" I asked.

He shrugged.

"Yes. My parents left me with her when I was five."

He frowned. "Left you?"

"Left me," I repeated. There wasn't anything more to tell. They were free spirits and hadn't wanted to be burdened with a headstrong, independent child so they dumped me on Aunt Velma's doorstep. "And you? Did you grow up with that white picket fence you're looking for?"

JT's jaw clenched. "No. My mother ran off with my piano teacher when I was six. My dad turned to alcohol and porn to ease the ache."

That sucked. I knew what it felt like to be left, but to be stuck with a disinterested parent was something different. Aunt Velma had never been disinterested. Crazy, but not disinterested.

"So you hate porn stars because your dad watched porn a lot?"

"I hate what it did to him." He sighed. "Goldie knew who I was the other day because my dad used to make me go into her store and pick up video rentals for him. She knew I was too young and dragged me into the back to talk to me about sex like she did to some of my friends who'd tried to rent from her. But she didn't give me the sex talk. She knew about my dad and that the movies were for him. Instead of having a minor walk into her store, she arranged it so the movies were left for me at her husband's doctor's office."

"She did that? That must have saved you tons of embarrassment," I replied. It was also really nice of her.

"Embarrassment? Are you kidding? Goldie's husband is an obstetrician. I had to go into a waiting room full of women who were pregnant or getting stuff looked at...*down there.* I was sixteen."

I couldn't help but laugh. "I guess that was how she gave you the sex talk after all."

"No kidding. Visions of pregnant women had me steering clear of sex for a long time."

"Porn isn't real, you know."

JT eyed me. "Huh. I didn't know that," he replied sarcastically. "Like you for example?"

"Well, Silky Tangles at least. It's her job. It's fake. She's an actress." I said those one after another as I ticked them off with my fingers on the steering wheel.

"You're saying I shouldn't be so hard on you because you're a porn star." It was my turn to eye him. "Fine. Fine. Your turn. If you don't like being in Bozeman, why come back at all? Where do you live anyway?"

I frowned. "Nowhere really. I had a place in LA, but that fell through earlier this month." I was not telling him about Roger. No way, no how. "I travel so much that I don't really have a place of my own. No furniture. No knick knacks. No picket fence."

"Don't you want one?" he countered.

I thought for a minute. "I never really thought about it, I guess, because I never had that. Aunt Velma's great and all, but she's...larger than life. That's why I went off to boarding school."

"It was so bad you wanted to go to boarding school?"

"When I got my period for the first time, I was fourteen. She not only had a period party and invited all my girl-friends, she invited the boys in my class as well."

JT squirmed at the use of the word period in a sentence not in reference to a portion of a hockey game. "Gotcha. No need to say more."

"I didn't really feel like I belonged anywhere. I guess..." I paused and sighed, lulled by the straightness of the road. "I guess I still don't. I don't have this dream I'm striving for like you do. I'm striving for...something, but I don't know exactly what it is. I'm thinking I'll know when I find it."

"Wow, that's really—"

"Holy fuck!" I shouted jumping up in my seat, but caught within the confines of the seatbelt. Something furry wound around my ankles, scaring the ever-loving daylights out of me, then claws dug into my leg.

I slammed on the brakes and held onto the wheel in a death grip as I steered the RV over to the shoulder of the road, the sound of the rumble strips on the white line irritatingly loud. A hiss and a meow from hell came from the floor by my feet. We stopped so abruptly we both jerked against our seat belts and something from the back hurtled through the air and hit the front windshield, shattering through it so it lodged just beneath where the rearview mirror should be.

A car whizzed by and honked its horn.

Tigger hopped up into my lap, gave a quick hiss, then

bounded over the arm rest and into the back. Both of us turned our heads to stare after the satanic animal as it pranced into the back bedroom.

"I thought Esther took that thing with her," JT muttered, breathing hard.

My heart rate was at stroke point, my adrenaline coursing through my veins so fast I was sweating.

JT turned his head to look at me. I looked to JT. Our faces were only a few inches apart, our fast breathing loud in the cabin.

"Are you okay?" he asked. The scar in his eyebrow was so pale in contrast to the little hairs. The whiskers on his cheek were on the way to being a beard. His eyes were so dark, almost black and they dropped to my mouth.

And then it happened. JT leaned in and kissed me, his lips warm and soft, his tongue dipping in as I gasped in not only surprise, but lust. It was unclear if it was the adrenaline that drove the insanity or perhaps the constant baiting, but the kiss definitely made no sense. But it felt...fabulous. I sighed and settled in, lifting my hands to tangle in his hair. He turned his head slightly and took the kiss deeper. When I made a little moaning sound at the back of my throat, JT pulled back. Stared at me. "Um...wow," he murmured, his voice rough. "I shouldn't have done that."

"I know," I panted. "Do it again."

Although I pulled his head in for more, JT quickly took over, kissing me the way he wanted, deep and lush licks, little nips on my bottom lip, thumbs caressing my cheeks.

After who knew how long, we both pulled back. The look of surprise on his face could be from either almost dying from impalement or the kiss. Both were adrenaline inducing, both brought about butterflies in my stomach, both made me a little sweaty all over.

"What was that for?" I whispered, ignoring his question. His lips were red and wet and he tasted...so good.

"I just...I just needed to know." He tugged on my messy ponytail.

"Were you kissing Daphne or Silky?"

He met my gaze, held it. "You. I kissed you."

That didn't answer my question at all because I didn't think he knew who I really was. A kiss didn't solve anything —it felt incredible, adrenaline inducing in its own special way—so I let the moment pass. Turning, I looked at the object lodged in the windshield, the glass a spiderweb of cracks around it. It was George the Gnome. The top of his pointy hat had pierced through the window and he was turned to face me, grinning.

JT undid his seatbelt, then ran his hand through his hair, over the back of his neck and stared at the gnome.

Eventually, he climbed from his seat and made his way to the back and peeked into the bedroom. The cat hissed and meowed and JT pulled the door shut behind him. Claws scratched at the door before they stopped, another angry hiss, then nothing.

"I told you that cat was feral. Holy crap, I may have peed my pants." I took a deep breath.

"Don't open that door."

Like he had to tell me that.

"Is there a reason why there are condoms scattered all over the bed in there?" He thumbed over his shoulder.

"Condoms? What are you talking about?"

JT shrugged. "All I know is that there are about thirty condoms strewn all over the place. Some box must have been overturned when we stopped short."

I bit my lip. "Goldie. Crap. Of course, they're Goldie's. I've heard she makes up boxes for people. Remember I told you about the one she made for her daughter-in-law, Jane. Matchmaking."

JT's eyebrows went up. "That's a lot of matchmaking. If we make it through all of those, I'd say we were well matched."

"If?" I asked.

"When, then. When we make it through all of those—"

"JT," I groaned. "Don't forget Tigger. How would you even get to them?"

He frowned, then grinned. "That cat's a cock blocker." He made his way back to the front, leaned forward and tugged at the gnome. "It's jammed in there good."

"Let's not take it out. We won't be able to drive with the air blowing in and I haven't seen any duct tape."

He looked at the gnome again, then agreed. "Do you want me to drive?"

"No. I'm fine now, I think. I just need to stop sweating so I can grip the steering wheel."

"Then I'm going to walk around and make sure everything's secure outside."

While he did that, I went to my bag and changed my pants. A taser didn't bring about an incontinent problem but a feral cat and a flying garden gnome did.

* * *

THE HIGHWAY STARTED to fill up with traffic, even in the middle of nowhere in Wyoming, all headed to Sturgis. Where we hadn't seen one motorcycle before, they were now on the road in droves. The RV wasn't quick moving to begin with, but our pace slowed the closer we got to the Rally. Traffic also slowed when it started to pass us, taking in the dents and scrapes, then the gnome in the windshield. We ate some of the chips Goldie had packed, but neither of us wanted to deal with making food, so we found a stop that had a gas station, a motel and a small restaurant that advertised it served breakfast all day.

We didn't talk about the kiss. We didn't talk about anything. That didn't mean I couldn't think about it and how crazy it had been. I didn't even like the guy! But man, he could kiss. I'd felt more in that short kiss than I had sleeping with Roger. Of course, it could be that it had been so long that my memory was poor. Either way, it made my nipples perk up and my lady parts come out of hibernation. But JT was ditching me in Sturgis for a woman named Sarah. A dentist who he figured could give him what he wanted. He wanted the whole picket fence thing, but he'd probably just end up getting sex. Most guys were fine with just that. JT would probably just be fine with that too, but he'd still go looking for it again with the next woman. Perhaps he just hadn't found the right one yet.

Perhaps I never found the right guy. Was it as simple as that?

I didn't have a chance to consider this because a group of six or seven Harleys pulled up, their engines loud.

They dismounted, then came over to us. "Dude, that's a shame about your bike," one guy said. They all were typical bikers, jeans, black boots, either a white or black t-shirt. One had a beard, another a handlebar mustache, another had a red bandana around his head. They stood around the trailer staring at JT's bike in mourning.

"It's getting fixed in Sturgis."

"What happened to your RV?" Another guy walked along the Titanic side and joined us by the trailer. "What the hell is stuck in your windshield?"

"That would be a garden gnome," I muttered.

I shouldn't have spoken up because the men shifted their

attention from the dead bike to me. "Holy shit, you're Silky Tangles."

"Dude, you lucky dog."

JT was getting his back slapped and I was getting ogled.

"We didn't know you were headlining in the area. Where's your show? The Ripe Peach?" Different men were talking and I couldn't keep up.

"Are you two stopping for lunch?"

"Yeah, join us."

"Shit, we're having lunch with Silky Tangles!"

Like a pack of wolves, I was culled from JT and led inside. The men were nice enough, courteous and thankfully kept their hands to themselves. They introduced themselves: Frank, Digger, Trey, Arty, Tom, Mike and Patrick. After about ten seconds, I forgot who was who.

Once inside, word spread like wildfire. I was placed in the middle of a large circular booth, three men on one side of me, four on the other. I wasn't going anywhere unless I wanted to slip beneath the table and crawl out, and I wasn't going to do that because it would give them some really pervy ideas.

JT stood at the table, hands on hips.

"Is he your manager or something?" one guy asked. I think he was Arty.

"Something," I replied. JT eyed me, probably trying to read my mind. I just rolled my eyes at him and shrugged my shoulders, which had him going over to a seat at the long counter, the waitress dropping a menu in front of him before wandering off.

"Please don't say he's your boyfriend, it would ruin it," Frank said hopefully.

"Ruin it?" I repeated, and I saw JT tilt his head to listen in. He wasn't far away. I felt safe, considering I was surrounded by a bunch of strange bikers. It wasn't the fact that they were bikers, it was more that they stood up for each other, like brothers, even if they were strangers. The guys who sat with me weren't the only bikers in the restaurant and I worried for JT. If someone did cross the invisible line, it would be him against a whole band of biker brothers.

"We know it's all an act, but I like knowing I've got a shot," added Tom.

I think I heard JT chuckle, but it was hard to tell.

"It's every guy's fantasy to be with Silky Tangles."

I felt myself flush, even though I wasn't her. "You know Silky Tangles is a stage name?" What her real name was, I had no idea, but no mother would strap her daughter with that from birth.

"How did you get into acting?"

"Is the guy John Boner really that hung?"

"Do you do yoga to get that flexible or are you double jointed?"

"Was it painful when you got your clit pierced?"

The barrage of questions was overwhelming, but the last one had me choking on a piece of toast. JT spewed his coffee —once again—and swiveled around on his seat to hear this answer.

The idea of a needle going anywhere near...*there* had me cringing. I thought of Goldie, who had the lowest embarrassment threshold known to man, where ridiculous questions and whispered talk slid off her like an egg in a Teflon pan. I could tell them I wasn't really Silky, but it wouldn't work. It didn't work on JT and he was jaded. These guys, well, I had them eating out of the palm of my hand. Figuratively, but I had no doubt they'd literally do it if I asked. So there was nothing to do but go with it. I envisioned what Goldie would say.

"It's not actually the clitoris itself that's pierced, but the little hood that covers it."

Every single man within a fifteen-foot radius stared at me. Coffee cups were poised halfway to mouths, silverware stilled, no longer cutting pancakes. JT's eyes flared with something a whole lot different than surprise. Even lust. It was a possessiveness I saw that had me taking a deep breath.

The waitress, who'd been refilling coffee cups, broke the silence. "So did it hurt? I mean, would you recommend it?" She bit her lip and eyed the other men, as if worried they'd judge her, but they didn't even look her way, just kept staring at me.

"I'd um...I'd talk to your doctor about that one. It's a big step." Yeah, a big step I had no interest in taking.

"Can I get a picture with you?" she asked.

Why a woman wanted a picture with me, I had no idea, but I just nodded my head. She pulled her phone from her apron pocket, handed it to a guy walking by the booth. She turned so she faced the camera and the guy got the shot.

"Thanks," she replied, then walked away.

"Can I get one, too?" The guy who took the photo asked.

Once they saw pictures were being taken, guys lined up for one of their own. I was allowed out of the booth to stand with my fans and JT volunteered to be the photographer, snapping one shot after another. Ten minutes in, my face was hurting.

"Thanks, Silky. I've already put this on my Facebook page. My friends aren't going to believe me when they see it," Arty said, phone in hand.

"Yeah, I tweeted my picture," Digger added, holding up his phone to show me the picture.

JT threw some cash on the counter and grabbed my hand. "Gentleman, it's been...interesting. Silky's got to be going." He put his arm around my shoulder in the way he'd done at the bowling alley. I just hoped these men were a little more civilized and I didn't have to punch any of them in the face.

"To answer your question from earlier," JT looked to Arty. "She's taken." JT kissed my forehead in a way that was gentlemanly, yet extremely possessive all at the same time.

All seven men stood, shook JT's hand with accompanying manly murmurs. *Way to go. Take care of her. Lucky bastard.*

They said their farewells to me, too. "Thanks guys, for lunch. You're all sweet."

JT tugged on my hand and we were out the door. "You put them in their place," he replied, smiling. "I didn't even have to do it."

"Oh?"

JT opened the door to the RV, let me climb in first.

"Sweet? No guy wants to be called sweet. That's *friend* territory."

"And where do they want to be?"

JT stepped closer so I had to tilt my head back to look at him. "Right here."

He leaned down and kissed me, cupping the back of my head in his palms, his thumbs brushing over my cheeks. This wasn't a *sweet* kiss. This kiss was an assault; aggressive and filled with all the frustration and anger over the past few days. It was also filled with all the lust that had been between us.

No matter how much I wanted to deny it, I was attracted to JT. He made me feel things I hadn't felt in a long time, perhaps ever. In fact, he made me *feel*. The men I'd been with in the past were safe choices; men who were sweet and I could leave them without a backward glance, without any heartache. It was safer to leave first. Even Roger. I'd used him at the end for his apartment alone. It had been easy to stay away from him because my heart hadn't been engaged. When I'd discovered he'd moved on with another woman, I was more upset I had no place to go than to have been dumped.

With JT, he made me mad, made me hot, made me feel for

the first time. I didn't know what to do about it, and the way he was kissing me, I didn't have the brain power to think about it. So I settled into the kiss. My nipples tightened, my skin heated and the way JT maneuvered my head this way and that as he wanted was very caveman of him. All he had to do was grab me by the ponytail and pull me into the back bedroom and that fantasy would be complete.

"Wait. Stop." I said against his lips. He moved to my jaw line with little nibbles and I swear I didn't intend for my head to tilt back to give him access to my neck and that deliciously sensitive spot behind my ear. "JT, we shouldn't be doing this."

"Why?" he murmured, his tongue flicking out to taste my pulse point.

"Because you're looking for the girl next door and I'm looking for...I don't know." I couldn't think straight when he fanned his breath along the shell of my ear and the sensation beelined straight for my hoohah.

"You're pushing me away now, aren't you, before you can feel anything." He didn't stop his attentions, thank God.

"I'm feeling an awful lot right now."

"Me, too."

Yeah, I felt a whole heck of a lot against my hip.

I grabbed the sides of his head, his hair silky beneath my palms and pulled his head back. JT's eyes were half-lidded with desire, a little frown marring his brow.

"We don't even like each other," I said.

"I'm liking you more by the minute."

"JT." I sighed. "You tased me."

"You punched me in the face." It was his turn to sigh. "Jesus, Daphne, I'm just starting to think you're not so bad after all."

I narrowed my eyes. "Why? Because I've got men falling over themselves to have me and you want to be first?"

He stepped back and I let my hands fall to my sides.

"That's pretty low. I've done nothing but protect you from those lunatic fans. I'd say I'm getting quite possessive of you. Do I want you for myself instead of letting any one of those guys have you? Hell yes."

"I'll be leaving again as soon as my next assignment comes in."

"You mean run away. Look, you're starting to like me and you don't like it."

"I barely followed that," I ground out. "Going to Sturgis and forgetting about life in the arms of Sarah *is* running away." I put my hands on my hips.

"I saw a family of four dead from a drunk driver." He ran his hand through his hair, his eyes switching from lust filled to bleak in a heartbeat. "That family was everything I never had and everything I want and now they're dead. If I want to forget for a little while, then so be it."

He stomped to the back of the RV, opened the door to the bedroom. Hissing and meowing had JT slamming the door shut.

"If a family—a *normal* family—is everything you want, then why are you kissing me?"

"Damned if I know."

CHAPTER 10

*A*ll along interstate ninety, cars and motorcycles passed us, slowing down and staring, then driving on. I drove for this stretch as JT was working his phone which was fine with me because his kiss not only stirred up feelings of lust that had been dormant, but stirred up old emotions too. An orgasm would be nice, a trip down memory lane was not. It didn't take a psychiatrist for me to know I had abandonment issues. My parents had left me when I was five. I could never live up to Aunt Velma since she was larger than life. I never measured up with anyone, never felt like I truly belonged, so I kept everyone at a distance. It was easier, safer that way. With a job that had me traveling all the time, it was easy to keep things simple. If things got tough, I just took the next assignment, the next plane out of Dodge.

But JT had messed all of that up. I missed the plane to Thailand and, using Goldie's line, everything went to hell in a hand basket from there. JT kissed me, Velma praised me, Esther had confidence in me enough to recommend me for a fill-in for the championship in roller derby, which she did not take lightly. Goldie entrusted me with her RV, which when I thought about it, wasn't saying much.

Because of the little taser incident, it had made me start to think about my life and I hated when I did that.

"You're not going to believe this," he muttered, breaking me out of my thoughts. "If you pull up your hash tag on Twitter, it's saying you're riding in a beat-up silver dildo shaped RV that has a horn out the front like a unicorn."

"It's not my hash tag," I replied. "I said it was a metallic pickle. Esther called it a dildo."

"Whatever," he countered. "You can't go incognito in this thing. No wonder everyone's honking at us."

My cell rang from my purse. "Get that, will you?"

JT pulled it out, looked at the screen. "Goldie," he muttered.

"Put it on speaker."

"What happened to the side of the RV?" she asked.

I glanced at JT. "What do you mean?" I asked warily.

"It looks like you struck an iceberg."

"Where are you?"

"A few hours from Fargo."

"Then how—"

"You've gone viral. That RV is all over Facebook and Twitter. Seriously, Daphne, if you wanted to go all stealth with this Silky Tangles thing, it's over now. The cat's out of the bag."

"Speaking of cats," JT said. "Tell Esther she forgot something."

"I'm not Silky Tangles," I ground out through clenched teeth.

"Whatever," Goldie said like a teenager. "Is that George the Gnome in the windshield? How on earth did it get there?"

"How viral are we talking?" JT asked, skipping the gnome question.

"You're just passing mile marker twenty-three in Wyoming."

"Holy shit," he muttered, not realizing the abilities of social media.

"I can't sell the RV with that damage," Goldie added. "It does look like a unicorn."

"You dented the front of it way before the iceberg incident," I countered.

She didn't respond for a moment. "Just don't let all this publicity slow you down. You've got to be here tomorrow night, remember. Velma and Esther are going to lose it if you don't get here in time." I heard grumbling through the phone.

"The traffic is terrible, so I'll try my best." We were still over an hour from Sturgis and the road was like LA at rush hour.

"All right, I'll let you go. But, Daphne, change your shirt. If you're going to be on Facebook, you need to at least show a little cleavage."

Goldie hung up and JT tossed my phone back into my bag and said, "She's right. A little cleavage would be good."

* * *

"THIS ISN'T GOING TO WORK," JT muttered as we pulled into a rest area for a pee break. It had taken us an hour to get fifteen miles. The Sturgis Rally was so popular, so big, the roadways were inundated. We'd just crossed into South Dakota, but at this rate, we were never going to make it to Sturgis.

Because of the traffic, I hadn't known we were being followed. This wasn't James Bond style followed, this was Silky Tangles style followed. When we parked at one of the in and out spots, so did about fifty motorcycles and a few cars.

"You can't go out there," JT warned. "I can't protect you in the ladies' room."

"I have to pee."

"Screw Goldie's rule on the stupid bathroom. No one's going to buy this wreck now anyway."

I glanced at the crowd outside, then at JT. "You're right."

I climbed from my seat and made my way to the tiny bathroom. When I emerged, JT was on the phone. "I know. Yes. You've seen it. It is not a unicorn horn, it's a garden gnome. Why?" JT was in the recliner, slouched in the way only men could. His tone was tired, but resolved. "Shit, I forgot about the bike. Forget it. I'll get it fixed when you get back home."

He threw the phone in his lap, looked up at me. "I locked the outside door, in case someone gets a little fan crazy."

"What's going on?" I asked, grabbing a soda from the mini-fridge. I offered it to him, but he shook his head. I sat down at the table.

"I can't leave you."

I popped the top and looked at him, eyes wide. "Some women would love to hear you say that to them."

He ignored my words. "This is insane. Have you looked out the window?"

I pulled down a slat on the metal blinds behind my head. "Oh, shit."

We were practically surrounded. Motorcycles and cars were parked every which way, people standing around talking, taking pictures.

"The traffic is only getting worse and once we get to Sturgis; it'll be so crowded you'll never be able to leave town. Hell, you'll never be able to leave the RV. This thing isn't very subtle. You can't fend off these fans yourself."

"I can just tell them I'm not Silky Tangles," I replied.

He gave me the look as if I had lost my mind. "That didn't work for me."

"You believe me?" I asked.

"Look, it doesn't matter if I believe it or not. It doesn't matter what I think about you or this situation. We've entered some alternate universe. I feel like I'm in *Planet of the Apes*."

I wouldn't take the situation that far, but then again, he wasn't the one who looked like a porn star. Well, he *looked* like a porn star, all hot and gorgeous and rugged and all, but people weren't showing his picture all over Facebook.

"We're not going to Sturgis."

I put down the can. "What? Why?"

"Because I can't let you deal with this on your own." He waved his hand around the RV.

"What about Sarah, the dentist?"

He sighed. "There's always a Sarah somewhere." I didn't really like the sound of that, but who was I to judge? I wasn't a hit with finding a man either—Silky's thousands of followers aside. "Besides, I was kissing you a little while ago, not Sarah, and I want to do it again."

"What are you saying?"

"We're going to Fargo."

* * *

By eight that night, we pulled into a campground in western North Dakota. Fortunately, the few other people staying didn't appear to be connected to the internet, or maybe there wasn't Wi-Fi, because besides strange looks at the state of the RV, no one recognized me. Also, good news was there were showers. I stood beneath the hot spray to wash off not only the miles of traveling, but also the night in jail as well. The rustic shower was infinitely better than the one in the RV where the bathroom was so small I couldn't lift my arms up over my head to wash my hair.

When I got back to the RV, JT was tilting a bottle of liquor into a hole he'd cut into the watermelon. "It's like being in college again," he said. His hair was still damp from his own shower. He'd changed into a pair of cargo shorts and a gray MSU t-shirt. His feet were bare and his smile was relaxed.

"How much have you had to drink already?" I asked. He looked too at ease with our situation to be completely sober.

"Let's just say I found Esther's secret ingredient." He grinned and I couldn't help but smile back.

I'd never seen him this way. Ever since the first time I saw him he was tense or aggravated or frustrated. Or all of the above. Moody JT was pretty hot, but laid-back JT was working for me, too. Once the bottle was empty, he pulled it from the hole and shoved it into the corner by the toaster oven. Yanking open drawers, he found a knife, then set to cutting a section off the rind, forming a great big bowl.

The knife was tossed into the tiny sink and he pulled two spoons from another drawer, handing one to me. Sliding in beside me at the table, he pulled the watermelon in front of us.

"Cheers."

He scooped out a piece of dripping watermelon and ate it. I watched as he grimaced, then swallowed. I took a chunk of fruit myself and put it in my mouth. The secret ingredient most assuredly was grain alcohol because I swear I breathed out fumes of jet fuel.

"Holy crap, that's strong."

"Slides down smooth," JT replied. "You know, I was thinking about your problem."

I arched a brow. "Problem?" Which one?

"Why don't you just get your own place in Bozeman? I mean, you're old enough not to live with Velma anymore."

I scooped up some more watermelon. "True."

"Your aunt is pretty crazy, but I'd think if you lived in town, but not *with* her, she'd be less...intense."

"Like Goldie, you mean."

He pointed his spoon at me, then poked the watermelon. "Goldie might be a little wacky, but you'll never hear me talk bad about her. The way she helped me with my dad—well, she went above and beyond. I won't forget that."

"Like how Aunt Velma took me in."

"You sound like you were an outcast or something."

The alcohol was starting to make my blood a little sludgy, my body relaxed, everything warm. And JT, he was starting to look mighty fine. "Not an outcast really, more like a cast-off."

"Have you seen your parents since?" He watched me closely, all of his usual angst toward me gone. At least for the moment.

"No. Last I heard they were in Europe somewhere. I'm sure Aunt Velma heard from them when I was young. I never asked, so she never told."

"It's not your fault they were terrible parents. It's also not your fault Velma's wacky."

I couldn't help but laugh at that. "She doesn't need any help from me to be crazy. She was that way before I was born."

"Then give her a chance. On your terms."

I swallowed another bite of watermelon. "What about you?"

He put his hand to his chest. "Me?"

"Yeah, you. Why don't you take a chance on someone who's not perfect?"

"No one's perfect, Daphne."

"Silky Tangles is perfect, because she's not real. Everyone can fantasize about her, love her. Wish they were with her in bed. But the real Silky is probably just this woman who has issues of her own and a really good stylist. Bad boyfriends, crazy relatives. She might even get PMS like the rest of us women."

JT cringed. "No way."

"Way. If I were Silky Tangles, wouldn't I look like this if I weren't on scene? Wouldn't I eat a liquored-up watermelon? Wouldn't I want to kiss a normal guy like you?"

JT's eyebrows went up. "You want to kiss me?"

I shrugged, modest all of a sudden.

"What's this about normal?" he kidded. "There are places on me I can guarantee *aren't* normal."

I bet. Oh yeah. I bet he was way more than normal in some places.

* * *

I AWOKE to the sun shining in my eyes. Wincing, I put the pillow over my head and sighed. It was then I felt the arm over my waist and a body spooning me from behind. The more I felt, the more I realized that it was *skin* I felt against me. Warm skin over very hard muscles. There was one other thing that was hard and it was pressing against my butt.

"Oh my God," I whispered, trying to slip out from beneath JT's arm. There wasn't much room to maneuver and I couldn't just slide off the bed. The mattress abutted the sides of the RV. As I turned to look at JT—whose naked chest had a very nice smattering of dark hair across it—his eyes weren't the ones staring back at me. Perched ridiculously on JT's hip was Tigger, watching me with his weird cat eyes.

I froze, hoping he wasn't going to hiss and dig his little cat claws into JT's hip and butt, even through the blanket. "Shoo,"

I whispered, flicking my fingers of one hand as I held up the corner of the sheet over me as best I could with the other.

Nothing. The cat didn't even blink.

JT stirred then, his eyes opening and awareness made them open all the way.

"Don't move," I said, my voice low.

He grinned. "No problem."

I rolled my eyes. "I don't mean *that*." I pointed at Tigger.

JT sucked in a breath and held it. "Go on, kitty. Nice kitty," he said in a nice, calm, soothing voice.

"Turn or something," I said.

"If I turn one way, he's going to poke holes in my ass with his claws. If I turn the other way—"

The cat hopped down off JT's hip, rubbed up against his blanket covered legs. I swear I heard it purr before it jumped down and went out the door.

We both exhaled, then I slammed the door shut, us on one side, the feral, schizophrenic cat on the other.

"This is a good sign, you shutting us in bed together." JT's voice was rough, his hair tousled, his eyes sleepy.

"We are naked," I hissed.

Now, he grinned. "I can see that." His eyes moved down my body. While the front half of me was covered with the sheet, the back half was completely exposed to him.

I hopped back on the bed and slid beneath the covers to hide.

"This is even better."

"Why are we naked?"

"I have no idea, but it works for me."

"You don't remember either?"

"The last thing I remember about last night was..." He thought for a minute. "We were talking about flour versus corn tortillas."

"Flour...wait, I do remember that. Then you said something about how cilantro was like eating fermented grass. Then it's all fuzzy from there for me."

"Esther's moonshine has some kick."

"Yeah, but right out of our clothes? JT, I hardly know you." My inner slut was fighting with the good girl within me. I turned on my side to face him, the sheet covering me up to my chin. Unfortunately, the more I tugged, the less that covered JT. Not that I was complaining, mind you.

"When put in difficult situations, people often get closer much faster than usual."

"This is a difficult situation?" I asked.

"We were almost killed by a flying garden gnome. I'd say it's outside of the norm."

I bit my lip. He had a point. "Last night, did we...um...what the hell happened?" I asked. I tried to remember, but there was a big blank area in the events after around nine o'clock.

"You'd know if we slept together," he replied, eyes dark.

I took a mental survey of my body. It didn't feel like I'd slept with anyone. "I don't think so."

JT moved so he was on top of me, surprising me and I didn't have a chance to get away. "When we sleep together, I promise not only will you be sure, but you'll remember it. Very well."

He lowered his head to kiss me, but I brought my hand up to cover his lips. "No way. I have the worst morning breath. Ever."

A smile formed against my fingers. He moved off me, which I was equally relieved and disappointed about. Before I could do anything, he tugged on my hip and pulled me back into him, then he turned us both so I was beneath him once again, this time face down. JT's body was lined up perfectly with mine—in every place—his forearms holding his weight off my body.

"There." He kissed the back of my neck, then started

nibbling down my spine, moving the sheet lower and lower as he went. "No morning breath problems. This position is going to work for me."

As one hand slipped beneath me to cup my breast, I had to agree with him. For once, we were both in complete agreement. "Oh yeah."

After he'd made me forget my own name by just playing with my nipple, he slid his hand down my torso and cupped my hip, pulling back so I was up on my knees.

"Oh my." It slipped out. Completely fell out of my mouth. Now both his hands worked over me, heating my skin as they went. "Why...why aren't we hung over?"

"Moonshine. It's good stuff. Goes down smooth." His mouth was at the juncture of my shoulder and neck and he bit down ever so lightly. His tongue flicked over the sensitized skin which had me crying out.

"Yeah, good stuff," I moaned, not talking about the liquor. His soft chest hairs tickled my back as he leaned over me and I arched my back into him. He slipped one hand between us, smiled against my neck. "Where's the clit ring?"

"Who are you in bed with?" I asked, then groaned. I needed to be sure he was in bed with me, not Silky.

"Daphne," he murmured against my nape. When he slipped his hand a little lower, finding me more than ready for him, he murmured, "This is something I'll never forget."

When he brought me to orgasm not once, but twice, I knew I wouldn't forget it either. If I'd known my sex life was in North Dakota, I would have visited a whole lot sooner.

CHAPTER 11

"There is no way you're getting out there and doing that," JT told me that night. His hands were on his hips, his hair falling over his forehead and he gave me a look that screamed insanity on my part.

He looked at me differently now. He no longer had the look of a man who wanted to tase me. Instead, he appeared very well-satisfied and had a gleam of possessiveness in his dark gaze. It was something to behold, especially when directed at me. I didn't want to jump him and tackle him to the ground and beat him up. I wanted to jump him and tackle him and have my way with him.

Perhaps that part, the sex part, was insanity. I'd slept with him after only knowing him such a short time. Did that make me slutty? Maybe, but at the moment I didn't care. I was actually falling for him and that was the craziest thing of all. I was falling for the guy who'd tased me.

I liked this caveman attitude, but I couldn't do anything about it at the moment. I was surrounded not only by Esther, Goldie and Aunt Velma, but the Roller Dolls were circling the track during their hour-long practice. We stood just outside the edge of the ring, a gust of wind tossed my pony-tail around every time the women circled, which was often and at very fast speeds. Music blared through the civic center's loud speakers and the lights were bright. The multi-purpose facility was set up for the roller derby, the angled ring laid out about the size of a basketball court.

"Look at them pushing and shoving, and this is just practice and they're all on the same team." JT did not look pleased.

"Chauvinistic much?" I leaned in and said into his ear so only he could hear. He wouldn't say a word about a bunch of guys in a football game.

He turned his dark eyes on me. "I protect what's mine," he growled, clipping the bike helmet onto my head and giving the clasp a little tug.

Holy hell in a hand basket.

Esther and Aunt Velma were happy—no, thrilled—to see me. I thought Goldie was pleased as well, but just because she didn't want to listen to her friends whine and worry any longer. The fact that the two of them held such hopes for me was a bit unnerving. They wore red Roller Doll t-shirts and were calling out tips and pointers in a slang only roller derby experts would understand.

"I've never done this before, you know," I reminded them, adjusting my elbow pads. I shifted from side to side on my skates, not used to having four wheels. It was a big difference from a narrow skate blade. I wore my black Capri yoga pants and one of my old t-shirts. It wasn't much for workout wear, but it would do for now. I'd get a uniform for the match tonight.

"You won the national championship twice for Pete's sakes," Aunt Velma commented. "This will be a walk in the park."

JT eyed me, surprised. "Hockey championships?"

I replied by holding up two of my fingers.

Esther came over to me and patted me on the arm just above my elbow pad. "You don't look as tense as you did earlier in the trip. What happened to all that angst? You need to tase her again." The last she said to JT.

"I think he tased her all right," Goldie said under her breath, eyeing me in an all too knowing way. I avoided meeting her eyes, so I watched the women doing some kind of drill instead. Fortunately, Aunt Velma didn't pick up on that and Esther was too worried about the roller derby game than to care about my sex life.

"You're worried that I'm not tense?" I asked Esther. "Shouldn't you be worried I don't know the rules?"

Aunt Velma waved her hand through the air. "It's not rocket science out there. Besides, you watched it enough on TV with me to know what's going on."

"I haven't," JT piped up.

"Okay, here's the short version. It's not a game, it's a match. There are five players on each team. A jammer, a pivot and three blockers. The jammer is the only player who can score points. The team gets a point every time a jammer passes one of the other team's players. To score a point, the jammer has to play fair and stay on the track."

"Daphne's not going to be a jammer, then." JT knew Aunt Velma and Esther well enough to know why they needed me.

Esther shook her head, her white curls still as stiff as ever.

"There's a two-minute period, called a jam, when points can be scored," Velma continued. "When the whistle blows, everyone leaves their designated start areas and skates around the track. The jammer is at the back so they need to pass everyone on the other team to get to the front and score. It's their teammates' job to help get them there."

JT listened as he watched the women go around the track. They wore bike helmets with red covers, like the one they gave me, elbow and knee pads, and various forms of skin-tight spandex covering the rest of them. This was an eclectic group. Some were skinny little things, others built like the ladies' German swim team on steroids. Some were young, some older, dark and light. Some had pink hair, others had tattoos covering their arms. JT would find it interesting just to watch without knowing the rules. If Velma tested him on what she was telling him, he might be caught out just ogling.

I was watching the ladies for a completely different reason. I was going out there with them and needed to ensure I had what they were looking for.

"I'm going to be a blocker," I told JT.

"You're going to be the enforcer, aren't you?" He turned to watch me as I wheeled back and forth, trying to stretch on wheels, his jaw clamped tight.

"Why, McCade, I didn't take you for a hockey fan. Of course, I'm the enforcer."

"Jesus, Daphne, the enforcer? Your job is to take people out. This is insane. Some of those women are huge." He cocked his head toward the ring.

I grinned at him. This was actually going to be fun. Yeah, there were a lot less pads involved, but I didn't have a stick and there was no puck. I just had to skate and elbow people. "Hip checking is my specialty."

"Just keep skating, and if someone gets near you later who's wearing a different colored uniform, take them out." Velma broke my role down to one sentence. "But save all the rough stuff for later."

"Got it." I skated onto the edge of the ring, letting the women practicing circle around past me. I did a few laps, getting used to the skates, watching as JT and Velma were talking, arms going every which way as if they were sign language interpreters. JT did not look happy. As I made the far turn, I saw a pleased gleam on Goldie's face. The whistle blew and I was pulled into the middle of the ring with the other women to huddle around the coach.

* * *

"Want to tell me what happened?" Goldie asked. I was in the ladies' locker room, unlacing my skates. Aunt Velma and Esther were off somewhere talking strategy with the coaches and JT wasn't allowed in. A few other Roller Dolls were still there, the remainder off getting some dinner.

I looked up at her from my bent over position. "I'm sorry about the RV. We ran into some troubles on the way."

Goldie waved her hand through the air making her gold hoop earrings sway. She wore her jeggings with a red t-shirt, although hers didn't have the Roller Dolls logo on it. At least she'd chosen the color to show spirit. "I don't care about the RV. What's going on with you and JT?"

I worked at a knot in the laces. "Nothing."

"Nothing? Really, Daphne, I'm not blind."

I just stared at her. "You can't tell anything happened."

She just shrugged. "It's not like the hickey on the back of your neck is invisible—not when your hair is up in a ponytail."

I automatically lifted my hand to the back of my head and sighed. "Fine. Something *did* happen, but nothing's going to come of it."

"Oh? I figured the box I left for you would help with that."

My mouth fell open. So she had been matchmaking. "Goldie, that was like thirty condoms." My voice dropped into a whisper. "We're not rabbits."

"Well, you better show him your Silky Tangles moves before that blind date shows up in Bozeman."

I sat up, stunned. I think my heart skipped a beat. "Sarah? In Bozeman?"

Goldie started fluffing her hair. "That's her name? I don't know much, but JT got a text from Bob that said Sarah still wanted to meet him. Since he—JT, I mean—wasn't able to make it to Sturgis, she'd come to him."

"Oh," I replied. I couldn't let Goldie see how the text bothered me, so I tugged off the skate and started undoing the other one. "See, I told you nothing's going to come of it."

"JT likes you, Daphne."

"He likes the fact that I'm Silky Tangles so he can use me and lose me. It's fine," I added when she was about to cut in. "I'm going to Brazil anyway. We both had our eyes open."

"Brazil?"

"I got an email from my editor with a great assignment in the rainforest." I tried to make my voice sound cheery. "Something about deforestation and the increase of cattle grazing land. It's a big article and I should be there a few months."

"You want to go to the rainforest for a *few* months? There's malaria and Anaconda snakes that eat people."

I pulled off the second skate. "It's my job, Goldie."

"Your job could be working at the Bozeman newspaper. Be an online blogger. Write for a local fishing magazine. You don't have to keep traipsing all over the world. Just settle."

I stood, put my skates up in one of the cubbies that lined a wall for later. "I can't just settle, Goldie. I don't know how."

She came to stand beside me. "You've been searching for a place where you belong for years. Practically your whole life. You're thirty years old, Daphne. You need to stop searching."

"But I haven't found where I belong yet," I countered, looking up at her through my lashes.

"You're never going to *find* it. You need to *make* it. Make the place where you belong."

"Like build a house or something?"

"Did Velma hit you in the head after that one time in fifth

grade?" Goldie asked, shaking her head in disappointment. "Rent an apartment, buy a house, build one. Whatever. *Just come home.*"

* * *

ESTHER AND AUNT VELMA had brought me some food while Goldie went off with JT to grab a bite themselves, then settle in their seats. I tried not to think about what Goldie had said, her words hitting pretty close to home. Had I been looking for a place I belonged all this time? Yes. Was I ever going to find it? Up until last week, I'd held out hope that I would. Now, I wasn't so sure. Now, Brazil sounded far away. Like if I went, I'd just long to be back in Montana. I'd never really felt this way before, doing everything I could to stay away from the state instead.

Why now? Why the sudden change? JT was certainly part of it, but we'd only known each other such a short time to say we'd have that white picket fence he wanted. But I'd slept with him, shared myself with him in ways I hadn't with anyone else before. And this road trip. God. I'd known it would be an adventure, but it had been insane. It made me realize that *life* was insane, not just Aunt Velma. What you did when it got crazy was what mattered.

When things got crazy, I got myself a man. A hot, cranky, lust-filled man.

"Nervous?" Aunt Velma asked.

I shook my head. "I'm fine, but I don't want to let you two down."

"All we want is for you to try your best," Esther said, surprising me.

"You don't care that I might make a fool out of myself or the team?"

"This is roller derby, Daphne, you're supposed to make a

fool out of yourself," Aunt Velma said. "Just kick some ass while you're doing it."

"Damn straight," added Esther. "Here." She held out a game jersey for me.

I held it up. It was a red and white striped t-shirt that looked like it would fit a twelve-year-old girl, but the fabric was stretchy. I turned it around to look at the back. "You've got to be kidding me," I ground out. "Sixty-nine?"

My number, sure enough, was sixty-nine. Both women grinned. And above the number was the name Silky.

"That's my roller derby name?"

"If the shoe fits," Esther said.

* * *

THE WOMEN LEFT me so I could change into the full Roller Dolls uniform: the sixty-nine shirt, a red skirt just like the field hockey players wore with little red bike shorts beneath, red knee highs. I felt like a cross between a candy striper and a waitress at a fifties drive-in restaurant.

When JT saw me in the outfit, his eyes widened in surprise before narrowing. "Holy shit, Daphne." He took my hand and tugged me along—easy to do since I was back on wheels, trying different doors on the lower level of the facility until he found one that was not only unlocked, but opened on a room that was empty. It turned out to be a storage room for the concession stand supplies. He shut the door behind him and pushed the button on the knob to lock it.

He didn't waste a moment and kissed me, pressing me against the cinder block wall. "You're really tall in those skates," he said, coming up for air. His hands started roaming over me, finding places that made me pant for him.

"I've never done it in skates before," I whispered as he

VANESSA VALE

licked and kissed my neck. "Oh, thanks for the hickey, by the way."

He pulled back and stared at me. Grinned wickedly. "My pleasure."

I rolled my eyes.

"How are we going to do this?"

He lifted me up off the ground, my ankles going around his waist, but there was no way I was going to get key articles of clothing off with the skates on.

"Shit," he muttered. Lowering me to the ground, he spun me around. With the wheels, I had to put my hands on the wall to keep from spinning all the way back.

"I've never done it with someone in skates before either, but I'm willing to give it a whirl." His hands started to work the little bike shorts down my legs. When he grabbed my hips and pulled back, I heard the crinkling of a condom wrapper, and knew I was in for one hell of a whirl.

CHAPTER 12

"There you two are!" Goldie called to us as we were working our way back to the ring to join the Roller Dolls. The stands were beginning to fill, music blared from the loudspeakers and an announcer was starting to amp up the crowd. It was time for the teams to warm up and skater introductions to be made. "Where have you been?" she asked, although the way she looked us both over, I had the distinct impression she knew.

"You have even less angst than before. What the hell is wrong with you?" Esther asked. In my roller skates, I was over a foot taller than she was.

"I'm fine," I told her.

"Fine? You're fine when the man you're canoodling with has a date with the woman from Sturgis?" she asked. She gave JT the beady eye.

He took a step back as if fearful.

"Tonight?" I asked. Goldie had said the woman was going to Bozeman. I knew nothing about tonight.

"No, not tonight," JT said.

"You're on the first flight out in the morning," Esther added.

The look on JT's face indicated Esther's death was imminent.

"Oh," I said. I felt...empty. Like something was missing. Like I was being left again. Wait, we had made no promises. We'd both said we wanted different things. I told all of this to Goldie earlier. But being faced with the reality of it, hearing from JT himself that he was heading back to Bozeman to meet another woman was something different. It hurt. Especially after what we just did in the supply closet.

"What about your bike?" Aunt Velma asked. She didn't have a warm and fuzzy look on her face either.

"Goldie's agreed to tow it back to Bozeman."

"I thought we were selling the RV," Aunt Velma said, looking to Goldie.

"Have you seen it? It can't be sold like that. Tomorrow, we'll just drive it home and take it to the scrap yard."

"I thought we were going to see the biggest rocking chair!" Esther added.

Goldie pursed her lips. "Esther, get a grip. The trip fell apart and we're going home."

The coach called to me to join the team.

"Come on, JT. Let's go find our seats. You can tell me all about this Sarah person."

I narrowed my eyes and thought mean thoughts.

"There's the angst-filled look. Go get 'em, tiger." Esther gave me a push on the back, rolling me in the direction of the team.

* * *

I SURVIVED. Actually, I did better than that. I knew I was considered the enforcer in ice hockey, being the brute who liked to roughhouse with players on the other team. But roller derby was a different experience entirely. It was...fun.

After the first hip check, I settled into my role, quickly learning the plays that got our jammer out to the front. The Roller Dolls won the match by fourteen points. During the two hours of play, I completely forgot about Brazil and JT and Sarah and Aunt Velma. I forgot about everything and just had fun.

The civic center was packed, the announcer stating that it was a sold-out crowd. Afterward, I celebrated in the center ring with the other Roller Dolls, even being asked to join them next season. When the owner of the team introduced himself, he thanked me personally for pulling in all of the fans.

"I'm not sure how I could have done that," I told him.

The man was in his fifties, portly, with thinning hair and a wide grin. "I've been following you on Twitter. It was marketing genius on your part having your trip here tracked by so many fans. I just didn't know you had such...diverse talents."

I lifted my brows and just stared.

"Announcing you were going to be in the match, well, it was the biggest turnout we've ever had. Can I get a picture with you? I promise to post it to your Twitter feed and Facebook."

He thought I was Silky Tangles. Why wouldn't he? "Can I get one of the back of your shirt, too?"

I smiled brittlely and spun around.

"You did it!" Aunt Velma yelled, coming over and pulling me into a bear hug. "I told you, Tony, my niece could fill in."

"An actress and a Roller Doll. It's quite a resume."

Someone called his name and he was off, pleased as punch.

"You told them I was Silky Tangles?" I asked, truly hurt.

This was worse than knowing JT was going to connect with Sarah. "I thought you were proud of *me*."

"Oh, honey, I've always been proud of you. But you have to admit, your followers really packed the stands. You not only helped win the championship, you helped bring new fans to the sport."

"I didn't do it," I countered. "Silky did." I couldn't stand there and argue with her. We were never going to see eye to eye. Ever.

I'd made it across the ring before Goldie called me. I braked and waited for her. She was flanked by JT on one side and a woman who looked an awful lot like me on the other. I had to look twice at her and then I realized who she was.

Silky Tangles.

"Daphne, there's someone here I want you to meet," Goldie said. "I'm guessing you know who she is."

I stared at my lookalike. It was remarkable how similar we were. Her hair, eye and skin color were almost identical to mine. Her hair was longer, but not styled like a beauty queen pageant as in her films. Her lips were fuller, but it could be the shiny lip gloss. I was taller than she in the skates, but we'd probably be the same height barefooted. Her breasts, well, they were definitely larger, although her clothes were fairly understated. Just a simple white V neck t-shirt and jeans.

"Wow, you're really pretty," I said.

Silky smiled at me. "I can say the same for you. You were crazy out there. I could never do something like that."

"Yeah, I'm a little crazy."

Was I the only one feeling a little awkward? Goldie was beaming and JT couldn't help but glance between the two of us.

"Goldie got in touch with me and asked me to come to the match."

"Really?"

"Someone pointed out all the Twitter and Facebook posts about my adventures on a road trip. I usually ignore stuff like that because the media's pretty crazy."

"I bet."

"Did you read about how I dated Channing Tatum?"

"I saw that," JT said.

"I thought he was married," I added.

"He is, or was. I've never met the man. So you can see why I blew it off at first. But then people started posting pictures of me—you—with them. A bunch of bikers in a restaurant, driving a weird looking RV, a rest area. All kinds of strange pictures."

"Mmm. Yeah, I'm pretty familiar with them."

"My manager called me to find out where I was because you do really look like me. I have to admit, the trip looked like tons of fun. I mean, you got to be with this guy," she added, putting her hand on JT's shoulder.

He smiled down at her and I saw red. No way was the real Silky Tangles getting her hands on JT. "Listen, Silky—"

Goldie came over and wrapped her arm around my waist. "Silky here is going to take over for you, Daphne."

"Take over what?" I asked. JT?

"Go change out of your uniform and Silky is going to meet with her fans, lead them away from you. She'll fly back to LA and all the media will go with her."

"You're off the hook," JT added. He didn't seem the least bit bothered by a porn star touching him.

"You've been a great boost for my ratings, so I owe you a thank you."

I smiled thinly. "Yeah, you've got quite the following."

"I do now, for sure. I'll dedicate my next film to you."

"That's not really necessary." Seriously. No.

It was time to go. I couldn't watch JT with her a moment

133

longer. "I should get changed. It was nice meeting you. Being you. Whatever."

I started to skate away.

"I'll see you in the fall when the movie comes out." I turned around at her words. "I'm going to do a signing at Goldilocks, so I'll be in Bozeman."

"Wow." I looked to Goldie, who was thrilled. "I won't be there. I'll be in Brazil for work. JT will, though. He's a big fan."

I glanced at JT who looked stunned. His mouth pinched into a thin line and he looked like he wanted to say something more, but didn't. Why, I wasn't sure. Perhaps it was because he had the woman of his dreams on his arm. A porn star he could love and leave. Perhaps it was because he knew nothing would happen between us and it was his way to end it. Perhaps it was because...well, who the hell knew?

* * *

GOLDIE HAD DONE A REALLY good job of seamlessly trading Silky Tangles for me. I'd skated into the locker room and swapped the candy striper outfit for my unexciting shorts and t-shirt. I pulled my hair back in a ponytail and slipped a baseball cap on my head. There weren't any fans waiting outside the door. There weren't bikers trying to get my attention. There wasn't anyone there but JT. He leaned against the cinderblock wall texting on his cell.

"Hey," I said, taking a deep breath, psyching myself up for this conversation.

He put his phone in his back pocket and smiled. "Hey yourself. You were...wow. Um...crazy out there. No, that's not the right word. Incredible, insane."

I grinned. "It was a lot of fun."

"Did you get hurt at all?" He looked me over for injury, although probably a little late.

I landed on my butt a few times, but I wasn't going to tell him that. "I'm fine."

"Hungry?"

"I'm okay. Where's Silky?" I asked, glancing around.

JT angled his head toward the main area. "In there signing autographs."

"I bet her fans are loving her now. Not only is she a porn queen, but she can also kick some serious roller derby ass."

"She's your number two fan," he said.

I frowned. "Oh? Who's number one?"

He pulled me into him so I had to tilt my chin up. "Me."

His mouth covered mine in a gentle, light kiss. "I think you scared ten years off my life when you were part of that group that went out of the ring."

"I barely fell down," I told him, remembering the moment well.

"No kidding. How you pulled that off, I'll never know. Shit, Daphne, I hope your roller derby days are over."

"Why?" I asked. "You're going to see Sarah soon and I'm off to Brazil."

"Right." He sighed. "What's this about Brazil?"

"A new story."

"When did you learn about it?" he asked, tugging on my ponytail.

"After the police station."

"Which one?" he asked. I knew he was trying to be funny, but it didn't come across that way. "Were you going to tell me about it?"

I looked down at the front of his shirt. "What does it matter? I was never a keeper for you. I was just a fantasy. Besides, I was always going to leave."

He frowned. "That's what you think, that I slept with you because I'm fulfilling a fantasy?"

"Of course. I'm fine with being your fantasy. I was never going to be your reality." I stepped back, pasted on a smile. "It's been...crazy. I'll see you around sometime."

Before I could cry—I never cried—I turned and walked away. When he called out to me, I just held up my hand then kept on going.

CHAPTER 13

*I*t had been a week since I flew back from Fargo. I'd had Aunt Velma's house to myself for the first few days as the Three Musketeers drove the RV back to Bozeman, leaving the broken bike at Bob's repair shop to be fixed when he returned from Sturgis. I spent the time sleeping and thinking, trying to figure out the mess of my life. It took me two days to realize my life wasn't a mess at all. It was just empty. I was filling it with writing assignments around the world to make it seem exciting, but I had no one to share it with, no one to come home to. I had Aunt Velma, she was always there, but her home wasn't my home anymore.

For two crazy days, I'd been on an adventure of a lifetime. I'd not only experienced it with Aunt Velma, but Esther Millhouse and Goldie as well. But they'd only been secondary to the excursion. It had been JT whom I'd travelled with. It had been JT to laugh at. Laugh with. It was a trip I would never forget.

He was a man I'd never forget.

"Are you sure you want to go?" Aunt Velma asked as I

packed my bag. The sloping ceiling in my upstairs bedroom was too low for her to stand upright, so she sat on the bed.

"Yes. I want to."

"Why, Daphne? Why are you going?"

"It's something I need to do."

"You mean it's a way to steer clear of JT." She gave me the one eyebrow up eagle eye.

"You want me to watch JT settle down with Sarah?"

"As far as I know, he hasn't even met this woman. You're writing off what's between the two of you."

"How do you know Sarah isn't here in town right now?"

"Goldie told me."

Then it had to be true. She knew everything.

"He thought I was Silky Tangles! I was just a fantasy for him."

Aunt Velma pursed her lips. "He's not an idiot. He knows you're not Silky Tangles."

"Of course, he doesn't. Now. He met the real deal in Fargo."

She picked up my pillow and fluffed it, tossed it back in place. "Look, he's got issues of his own, of course, but not everyone's going to leave you."

I dropped the socks I'd been holding. "What?"

"Sit down." She waited until I did so, the open suitcase between us. "Your parents. I wanted to kill them for leaving you. But instead I thanked them daily for leaving you. I got *you* because they were so selfish. I know you think I'm crazy, but I never left you. Never."

My throat hurt with tears. "I know, but you're larger than life, Aunt Velma. I can't compete."

"Oh, honey, you never have to compete with me. Everyone loves you for being you. Even JT."

My head whipped up at his name. "He doesn't love me. He doesn't really even know me."

"That's not his fault, it's yours. If you like him, then stay. Let him get to know you. Don't run away because he just might stick."

I wiped at my eye. "I've been back a week and he hasn't been by. It's over."

Aunt Velma sighed, then stood up, at least as far as she could. "What time's your flight?"

"Two."

"I'll say goodbye now then since I have to meet Esther. Her car's broken and she needs to take Tigger to the vet to get spayed. Then we're meeting Goldie for lunch. She's taking George the Gnome back to Zach this morning."

The thought of the gnome had me smiling. I would never forget how it flew into the windshield. I would never forget the kiss that followed.

* * *

I WAS LATE. Again. I'd forgotten to get gas so the Rabbit's fuel light came on and I had to stop. By the time I was flooring it down the Frontage Road toward the airport, I only had an hour before my flight. This time, when I was pulled over for speeding, I wasn't surprised, although that didn't keep me from swearing.

Scrambling for my purse, I pulled out my license and reached into the glove box for the registration, not noticing the police officer standing beside the car.

"I see you know the process," the man said. I whipped my head around when I recognized his voice.

JT.

"You look familiar," he said. He wore his reflective aviator sunglasses once again so I couldn't see his eyes. His body was the same: big, virile, rugged. The MSU t-shirt fit across him snugly and the gun on his hip looked just as hot as last time.

"Yeah, I get that a lot." I tried to calm my racing heartbeat at just the sight of him. I could even *smell* him through the open window and it brought back a flood of memories. My mouth watered wishing I could just taste him again.

"Step out of the car, please."

"JT, I don't have time for this. I have a flight to catch."

"Ma'am, step out of the car."

I rolled my eyes and sighed.

Climbing out, I put my hands on my hips.

"Where are you traveling to this time? Brazil?"

"Minnesota."

He paused, not expecting that answer. "What?"

"I said, Minnesota."

"I thought you were going doing a story in Brazil. What's in Minnesota?"

"A hockey team reunion."

He took off his sunglasses and hooked them over the neck of his shirt.

"I'm surprised you're working. Shouldn't you be showing Sarah around town?"

"I'm not working. I'm pulling over a speeding driver."

"Why?" I asked, completely confused. "Why are you pulling people over?"

He put his hands on his hips. "I'm not pulling people over. I'm pulling *you* over. Jesus, Daphne, I don't want you to go."

My mouth fell open. "What?"

"Don't go to Brazil. Don't leave Bozeman. There's something between us, something crazy." He ran his hand through his hair. "We should give it a shot."

"How did you know where to find me? You want to...wait." I held up my hand. "What about Sarah? The white picket fence?"

"You said it last week. Sort of. You said you were my fantasy, but you were looking for reality."

"Yeah, I remember." I remembered all too well.

"You had it backwards." He stepped into me so he blocked the sun, tucked my wayward hair behind my ear. "Sarah and the white picket fence were just fantasies. *You* are my reality."

"Holy shit."

He grinned. "Yeah, holy shit. Now can you please not go off to Morocco or Mozambique or Minnesota."

"I was only going to be gone for the weekend. I... I rented a little house downtown."

JT grabbed me and pulled me into his arms, hugged me to him so tightly I couldn't breathe. Or maybe it was the fact that the stupid wall I'd built around my heart crumbled and I was, for once, letting someone in. "I'm still going to take assignments, shorter ones, but only for a little while longer. Goldie's idea about working for a local magazine was a good one. I've started putting my resume out there and I should hopefully hear from one of them. In the meantime, I've got money saved up."

He pushed me back, only just enough to look down at me. "So if I don't tase you, you'll give us a try?"

I nodded. "Will you?"

"As long as you don't punch me in the nose."

"It's a deal."

NOTE FROM VANESSA

Don't worry, there's more Small Town Romance to come!

But guess what? I've got some bonus content for you with Daphne and JT. So sign up for my mailing list. There will be special bonus content for each Small Town Romance book, just for my subscribers. Signing up will let you hear about my next release as soon as it is out, too (and you get a free book...wow!)

As always...thanks for loving my books and the wild ride!

GET A FREE BOOK!

JOIN MY MAILING LIST TO BE THE FIRST TO KNOW OF NEW RELEASES, FREE BOOKS, SPECIAL PRICES AND OTHER AUTHOR GIVEAWAYS.

http://freeromanceread.com

ABOUT THE AUTHOR

Vanessa Vale is the *USA Today* Bestselling author of over 40 books, sexy romance novels, including her popular Bridgewater historical romance series and hot contemporary romances featuring unapologetic bad boys who don't just fall in love, they fall hard. When she's not writing, Vanessa savors the insanity of raising two boys, is figuring out how many meals she can make with a pressure cooker, and teaches a pretty mean karate class. While she's not as skilled at social media as her kids, she loves to interact with readers.

www.vanessavaleauthor.com

Their Runaway Bride

Their Kidnapped Bride

Their Wayward Bride

Their Captivated Bride

Their Treasured Bride

Their Christmas Bride

Their Reluctant Bride

Their Stolen Bride

Their Brazen Bride

Their Bridgewater Brides- Books 1-3 Boxed Set

Outlaw Brides Series

Flirting With The Law

MMA Fighter Romance Series

Fight For Her

Wildflower Bride Series

Rose

Hyacinth

Dahlia

Daisy

Lily

Montana Men Series

The Lawman

The Cowboy

The Outlaw

Standalone Reads

Twice As Delicious

Western Widows

Sweet Justice

9 781795 900133